Christmas

In

Florence

Joanne

Fisher

ACKNOWLEDGEMENTS

Published in the United States of America, in the year 2020, by Joanne's Books. www.joannesbooks.com

ISBN: 978-1-7923-4004-8

Book Cover by: Macred Designs

https://www.robin-mcdonald.com/home.html

Edited by Daniel B. Fisher

DEDICATION

I am dedicating this book to the beautiful, clean, and historical city of Florence which I had the pleasure of visiting multiple times when I lived in Italy. Every time it was a sparkling experience. And to the people of Florence, I say— or better yet, I sing, "Firenze lo sai, non è servito a cambiarla, la cosa che ho amato di più è stata l'aria..." (Florence you know, no use changing her, the thing I loved the most was the air...) Ivan Graziani, 1980. YouTube: Firenze Lo Sai

CHAPTER ONE

January 2020

"Hey, Ma, guess what! I found a job!"

"Oh, Dante, that's wonderful! I'm so happy for you!" Sofia hugged her son. "Now, sit and tell me all about it while I make some espresso."

Dante sat down and noticed a batch of biscotti that his mom had just pulled out of the oven. "Mmmm...hey Ma, can I have one?"

"Of course, Dante, go for it." She set up the espresso pot, turned on the heat and went to sit next to her son. "Now, tell me all about it." Her smile stretched from ear to ear.

Dante had graduated from Humber College in fall of 2019 and had been searching for his career position ever since. He had many offers, but he wanted to find a position where he could travel to Italy. He was interested in perfecting his Italian. Even though he grew up in Woodbridge, he still spoke very little Italian. In fact, all he spoke was Calabrese dialect, which he used when talking with his grandmother, Nonna Teresa. Since she had passed away in 2018, his opportunities to speak the language had diminished drastically.

Sofia was so proud of her Dante. He was the eldest and most responsible and dependable of all her children. She really wanted him to be happy, but she would have preferred that he have a job that allowed him to live closer to her. However, he didn't want that. Ever since middle school, he had desired to fly the coop.

"All right, well this company is called LCD which means Leather Commerce Distributor, and they are located in Calgary."

"Calgary? That's so far away, Dante."

"Ma, I'm not going to Calgary, it's just their headquarters. They have offices all over Canada, all right?"

Sofia nodded and kept quiet.

"They basically sell hides to companies all over the world that produce leather goods like jackets, handbags, shoes, and so on."

"Shoes? You've piqued my interest."

Dante rolled his eyes. What was it with women and shoes? "Anyway, they were looking for a point of contact to travel to Italy, and since I'm Italian, they hired me."

Sofia didn't know whether to laugh or cry. So, she frowned, instead. "Italy, huh?"

"Ma, come on, you knew I was looking for something like this. I want to travel, and I want to become fluent in Italian. This is exactly what I have been looking for. I've told you this over and over." He was losing his temper at his mother's overprotectiveness. She always got this way with him.

"I know, Dante, I know. but you know how it is. We are Italian and we don't like our kids leaving home. Not now, not ever." She sipped her espresso. "But I understand that you have always wanted to leave, so now's your chance. Bravo!" Her voice dripped with sarcasm.

Oh, here we go with the guilt trip! He was also fed up with the dreaded guilt trip!

"Ma, come on, I'm gonna be thirty this year!"

"Yeah, yeah, thirty…" She smirked. "So, when are you leaving?"

"Beginning of February."

"So soon?"

"Yeah." He cracked a smile. The excitement made his eyes light up. "I got a feeling that 2020 is gonna be a hell of a year!"

"That's it? You're just gonna leave? Don't you need training or something?"

"Yeah, I'm goin' to Calgary next Tuesday to begin my training."

"Sheesh, Calgary? That's so far away, Dante. What am I gonna do without you all these weeks!" She was already dreading the distance between them.

"Come on, Ma! You got Gianna and AnnaBella. You're gonna be fine."

She got up and stood right in front of her son. "Yes, I know but you…you are my only son and I have never, ever been separated from you. You know that, right?" she was close to having a nervous breakdown.

"Ma, please don't make this harder than it has to be. Please?" He hugged his mother. "You're not losing me, Ma; I'm just flying the coop, that's all. I'll come back to visit now and then. You'll see."

She wasn't convinced. She scoffed at him, turned, and sat down, again, in front of her espresso. As she sipped, she pouted.

Dante left the kitchen. He couldn't take any more of his mom's overreactions. She was overbearing, to say the least. He knew so very well that she loved him, but he never understood why she smothered him like she did. "It's an Italian thing," she would say to him, but he still could not handle it. He looked at the bright side: in a few days, he would finally leave his mother's grip. And he was going to make sure it was for good! He could not tell her, though. That certainly would break her heart. It's not that he didn't love his mother—he did. He simply could not pass the rest of his life being checked up on, appearing in her selfies, and called and texted constantly. He also did not tell her that he would be going from Calgary directly to Italy. He would not be stopping in Woodbridge. Only if his plane connected in Toronto, would he consider leaving the airport, visiting his family for an hour or so, and then taking the connection to Italy.

Gianna bumped into Dante as they crossed paths in the back hallway. "Oh, hey Bro! 'S'up?" she was in a good mood.

"Mom." he rolled his eyes. "I can't wait to leave." He whispered in his sister's ear.

"Well, you are her favorite." She peered at him.

"I know…I know…but still…"

"She'll get used to it; you'll see."

"Man, I hope you're right, Sis." He opened and closed his hand to indicate he wanted her keys.

"Here you go, Bro…don't crash it!" she slapped the keys into his palm like a nurse handing an instrument to a surgeon.

"No way, Sis! I don't want your insurance to go up—again!" he smirked.

"Uggh! I hate you!"

"Love you, too!" he yelled from the driver's seat as he took off in his sister's Subaru Impreza.

"Gianna, is that you?" Sofia yelled from the kitchen.

"Yes, Ma, it's me." Gianna walked into the kitchen, holding her phone and texting.

"Where's Dante?"

"He went out," she said distractedly.

Sofia finished washing the espresso cups, dried her hands on her apron, and pulled her phone from her apron pocket. "Where did he go? Let me find out." As she began texting, Gianna snatched the phone from her.

"No, Ma! You can't keep texting him. He's really getting annoyed with you." She set her mom's phone on the kitchen table. "Sit!" She was about to give her mom a lecture that was long overdue.

"Ma, he loves you, he does. But you have to stop bugging him all the time! He's not your baby, anymore. He's twenty-nine, for God's sake!"

"So, just because you guys are technically adults doesn't mean I have to stop worrying about you."

"I know, but the problem is that you ONLY worry about Dante and don't give a crap about me and AnnaBella!"

"That's not true!"

"Yes, Ma, it is. But you know, we don't care that you prefer Dante over us. It's just that you've got to stop being

6

overbearing with him. You are pushing him away. Why do you think he wants to go to Italy? He wants to get as far away from you as he possibly can. Don't you see?"

"No, no. I'm not doing that—am I?"

"Yes, you are. Nonna started it and you're continuing. You have to tone it down or he will never come back. You gotta let him live his own life."

"Yeah, I guess you're right." She picked up her phone.

Gianna pulled her phone down a bit. "And it starts with the text messages and phone calls. Limit yourself. Try sending only three text messages per day and then only two and finally only one. It's like breaking a bad habit. A little at a time."

"Three, eh?"

"Yep, three. Try it. Starting now." She gently pulled her mom's phone out of her hands. "Let me see how many you've sent him today." She checked the text messages to Dante. "I see one, two, three, four already today and it's only three in the afternoon." She shook her head. "Tell you what. Only one more text for today, so you'd better make it good."

"One more?"

"Yes, Ma."

"Just one?"

"Yes, Ma."

Sofia blinked rapidly and looked at her daughter with puppy dog eyes.

"No, Ma! You've got to make an effort here!"

"All right, all right…geez…you're a little dictator, ya know?"

"Me? Oh, that is so rich! I learned from the best!" Her eyes met Sofia's. "One more text and that's it. I'm gonna look at your phone and if you send more than three per day, I'm taking your phone away from you!"

"Well, look how the tables have turned. When all three of you were younger, Daddy and I would take the phones away from you. And now look."

"Well, if you hadn't abused your motherly privileges, all this wouldn't have happened."

"What wouldn't have happened?" AnnaBella walked in wrapped in a robe with her hair rolled in a towel. She opened the fridge door and pulled out a San Pellegrino.

"I'm trying to get Ma to stop smothering Dante."

"Ha! Good luck with that!" She went into the living room and sat on the couch while playing with her phone.

"Oh, you think I can't do it, eh? Well, I'll show you! I'll show both of you!" she took her phone from Gianna's hand, took off her apron, slammed it on the counter, and headed upstairs, stomping with each step.

Gianna proudly walked up to her sister and gave her a high-five. AnnaBella smiled and winked. Gianna sat next to her sister. "Do you think she'll do it?"

"Not a chance!"

"Yeah. I know, right?"

Sofia was sitting on her bed, frowning. "Why did I agree to that stupid bet? What was I thinking?" she shook her head and swiped her phone to unlock it. She looked at the messaging. Nothing from Dante. "Oh, he's probably out with some Canadian slut!" She rolled her eyes and began texting Dante.

"Sofia?"

"In here, Santo." She pressed and held the backspace to erase the text. She would send it later.

"What are you doing in here all alone?" Then he scrutinized her face. "What's wrong?"

Sofia shook her head, but her expression gave her thoughts away.

"What did Dante do now?" he asked. Dante was always up to something, and Santo knew very well that his wife had a tendency to cover up their son's shenanigans.

"He found a job," she muttered under her breath.

"A job? Nice!" but the look on Sofia's face said otherwise. "No? Why?"

"He's going to freakin' Italy!" Tears burst forth.

Santo sat next to his wife and held her tight. "Come on honey, it'll be all right." He cradled her while she wept. "He's twenty-nine. He's gotta fly the coop eventually." He kept on rocking her, but the weeping continued. "I know he's your firstborn and that he has a special place in your heart…" he tightened his embrace a bit. "…but he needs his freedom. He must learn about life. He must make his own mistakes if he's ever going to be a man. You understand that don't you?"

"No. Yes, I understand…I guess." Her sobbing had morphed into sniffling.

Santo reached over and grabbed a tissue from the box on the nightstand. "Tell you what…" still holding her tight. "we'll go visit him when the weather gets better. Maybe May or June. What do you say?"

She loosened herself from his embrace to look him in the eyes. "Really? Do you mean it?"

"Yes, I mean it. We haven't been to Italy in years, so we're due for a visit." He smiled, hoping for her return smile.

"Oh, Santo! You're amazing!" she cracked a smile, then hugged her husband and kissed him all over his face— of course, ending in an extremely passionate lip lock.

"Oh, well, remind me to take you to Italy more often." He kissed her again as he pulled her down onto the bed.

CHAPTER TWO

February 2020

Dante felt the bump as the airliner's wheels settled onto the runway. He lurched forward against the seat belt as the jet slowed. As it turned off onto the taxiway, the chief flight attendant announced, "Welcome to Fiumicino "Leonardo da Vinci" International Airport in Rome. Local time is four PM, and the temperature outside is 11 degrees Celsius. Please remain seated with your seat belts fastened until the aircraft is fully stopped at the gate." As it was a Canadian airline, the announcement was repeated in French.

Dante waited patiently for the family sitting in his row to collect their things. He had been waiting patiently throughout the entire flight, but now he was becoming antsy.

"Boy, that was a long flight!" The young woman next to the window was also patiently waiting for Dante to grab his carry-on bags and get out of her way. He had been using all his best pick-up lines the entire flight. She had to feign sleep in order to get him off her back.

"Yeah, very long flight," she said sarcastically.

Dante got the message loud and clear. "Well, you take care now, Amy. It was nice meeting you," he said to her as they got on the jetway.

Amy didn't even acknowledge him. She whipped around him and was out of his sight before you can say, "See ya!"

"Huh," he whispered to himself.

He followed the crowd through the jetway, into the main terminal area. He looked for the exit signs, but there was no need for that; he simply followed the crowd. He saw TV monitors all over the terminal, all tuned to the same channel, Rai International. Just like home. Only one channel; the one they want you to see. He saw the current story about the mayor of Florence, Dario Nardella, initiating Hug a Chinese Day and giving a Chinese man standing right next to him, a warm embrace.

"Huh, I wonder if that Chinese dude speaks Italian?" he whispered to himself.

Dante slid his passport back into his front pocket. "Molte grazie." and headed for the luggage carousel. He was enjoying this trip to Italy so far.

"I can't believe how gorgeous these Italian ladies are!" he exclaimed as the guy who had sat next to Dante on the plane approached.

"I know, right?"

The carousel started moving with a jolt. It squeaked and squawked in an exceedingly shrill manner. Dante almost had to cover his ears. Wow, that thing needs some maintenance!

"So, are your relatives coming to pick you up?" Nico asked as he diligently searched for his luggage.

"Yes. At least I hope so."

Nico forcibly hauled a dark gray suitcase from the carousel and plopped it by his side.

"What about you?"

"Oh, I don't have relatives here in Rome. I'm renting a car and heading for Sicily." As a red and black duffle bag with a Milan logo approached, Nico grabbed it and hoisted it onto his shoulder.

"Milan? Dude, really?" Dante asked.

"Dante, I've been a Milanista all my life. Not changing now."

"Ha-ha! I've been a Juventino all my life."

"Okay, well, I'm outta here!" He shook Dante's hand before he yanked the handle on his suitcase to roll away. "Nice meeting you. And good luck at your new job!"

"Yeah, same here...even if you are a Milanista..." Dante said loudly so Nico could hear.

Nico waved his hand in the air. He hesitated for a moment, then turned to fact Dante. "Oh, if you ever want to

13

come down to Sicily, you're welcome to come. You have my number, right?"

"Yes, I do."

"All right then, don't be a stranger and I promise you'll be welcome even if you are a Juventino!" Nico waved again and disappeared among the crowd.

"Nice guy," he whispered to himself while his black and white suitcase was making its way toward him. "Ah. One down; one to go." His mom had bought him a 3-piece Juventus luggage set as a bon voyage gift. Fond memories entered his mind even if they were very recent ones. He saw the smaller suitcase approaching. "And here's the other one." He pulled both handles up and rolled them alongside himself, as he made his way to the terminal exit.

"Eccolo! Dante!" Alfredo yelled out waving feverishly at his nephew.

"Oh, Zio Alfredo, ciao!" Dante picked up his pace as Alfredo met him at the end of the blocked off aisle.

"Dante!" he hugged his nephew and double kissed him. "Come stai?" and hugged him again.

"Bene, bene." Dante didn't have a large Italian vocabulary, but he was working on it. As he grew up, he had learned only the Calabrese dialect, along with some Italian words. However, when he was hired on for this new job, one of the requirements was to speak Italian fluently.

Alfredo extended his arms to look at Dante. "Ma che bel uomo che sei diventato!" he complimented him.

"Grazie Zio," blushing a bit. Dante felt awkward receiving compliments from another man, even if it was his uncle.

His uncle continued in Italian. "Come, let's go. I parked a good distance away, so we have some walking to do."

"That's okay Zio. I don't mind walking."

"Of course! You're young! You can walk. Not like me...oy...old age is such a disappointment! It's not for lightweights," he lamented.

"Come on, you're not old!" he really didn't want to offend his uncle. He didn't know him that well, and wasn't very comfortable opening up just yet.

"Ah! I like you already!" Alfredo patted Dante on the back as he took the smaller suitcase from him and began to roll it.

Dante shrugged his shoulders with a satisfied smile and followed his uncle. They walked through the airport which seemed to be endless, going up a few escalators, and finally taking an elevator which brought them up to the fourth level parking lot.

"Here we are." Alfredo took a right, followed by Dante, but they didn't arrive at Alfredo's car for what seemed a couple of miles.

"You weren't kidding, Zio."

"I wasn't." Alfredo stopped behind a blue Citroën C4 Picasso. The car clicked as he placed his right foot under the exhaust and the rear hatch lifted automatically.

"Oh, mom's car does the same thing," Dante smirked.

"Oh? Your mom has a Citroën too?"

"No. We don't have Citroëns in Canada. She has a Honda."

"Ah, I see."

"Yes, and it's much larger, too." He looked around in the airport parking lot. "I see that all the cars are so tiny here."

"Yes, well America is America, and all is much bigger there."

"Zio, we're not in America you know. We're in Canada."

"Ah! Same thing! Here in Italy, all is America. Come on. Let's go, Dante!"

As Alfredo drove out of the airport, Dante offered to pay for parking. But Alfredo would have none of it.

"Thank you for this, Zio, but you do realize that I'm going to be living with you and I don't want to be a burden. I've decided to pay you some amount of room and board."

Alfredo was shaking his head.

"No, Zio! Come on, it's not fair to you and Zia!" His mother's words were echoing in his head from her lecture a few days before he left.

"Dante don't let your aunt and uncle convince you otherwise. You must pay your fair share. It's only right."

"Yes, Mom, I will. I promise." He was missing his mother, already.

The drive into Florence was stunning. The rolling hills of the Tuscany countryside were the perfect balance of trees, grapevines, and farmland. Even though it was still winter, the landscape was colored pale green, indicating a spring that was impatient to bloom.

"I must say, it is beautiful here."

"Yes, it is. This scenery is famous all over the world."

"We still have snow on the ground back home."

"That's some long winter!"

"Yes, it is but we're used to it."

A familiar tune began to play on the radio.

"Is that Zucchero?"

"I believe so."

"Mom and Dad love him. She went to see him in concert last year."

"We do too but we haven't seen him in concert. Maybe this year we will."

Alfredo turned onto Via Delle Cinque Giornate and pushed a button on what seemed like a garage remote. "Here we are." The huge, metal gate parted inward in the middle and Alfredo drove into a courtyard with several balconies attached to the buildings that looked onto the courtyard. Another garage door opened, and Alfredo drove in and parked his car. "Here we are. Home sweet home."

Dante got out of the car as the Citroën's hatchback opened. He pulled out his luggage and turned to his uncle, his eyes asking, "Where to?"

"Over this way." Alfredo pointed to a double-panel glass door. "Come." He slid open one panel to let Dante in.

Dante wheeled the luggage in and faced a long stairway. He wondered why his uncle hadn't opened the other half of the door so he could walk in without wheeling in one piece of luggage at a time. That seemed odd to him. He picked up the two suitcases and started climbing the stairs.

"Dante! Dante!" his aunt Giuditta yelled at the top of the stairs! She descended a few stairs to meet him and hug him.

He was a bit flustered with the luggage and trying to hug his aunt, but he did his best. "Ciao Zia! How are you?"

Giuditta gave him four kisses, two on either side of his face. "Come, come, I made lunch. Come." She reached for one of his suitcases. But when she felt its weight, she left it in Dante's capable hands. "Oh, you have them already."

Dante followed her into the apartment. There were only two apartments on the third floor and Giuditta guided him into the one on the left. As he walked in, he could smell the distinct and mouth-watering aroma of Penne Strasciacate. "La mamma è qui?" he was a bit worried that perhaps, somehow, his mother had secretly followed him to Italy.

"Ma cosa dici? Perchè questa domanda?" his uncle asked.

Whew! He thought. "Niente, niente." He put his luggage down.

"Ah, you smell the Penne, do you?" his aunt asked him in Italian.

"Yes, Zia, I do and for a second I thought my mom had played a trick on me."

Everyone in the room laughed loudly.

"Come. I'll show you your room." Alfredo patted his nephew on the back. "Riccardo will be here tomorrow to see you."

"He doesn't live with you?" Dante followed his uncle to one of the doors in a long hallway. This is it? He thought. Boy these Italian apartments are tiny.

"No, he lives in Cuneo." He opened the bedroom door and went straight to the armoire, which he opened for Dante.

"Cuneo? Where's that?" he asked as he rolled in his suitcases and dropped his carry-on onto the twin bed.

"It's in the north, close to Torino." Alberto pulled down on the flat rope that was next to the window, bringing up the shutters and letting the sunlight in. Then he opened the window.

The pair began walking down the narrow hallway.

"Torino? You mean the Torino where Juventus plays?" His heart skipped a beat.

"Oh yes, exactly. That Torino."

"Wow! Has Riccardo ever seen Juventus play?" he followed his uncle back out to the dining area.

"Oh yes, he has. Several times."

"That's amazing! I can't wait to go visit him up there."

They reached the kitchen.

"Well, perhaps later. But for right now, let's eat." He pointed to an empty chair.

Dante sat down while his aunt placed a heaping plate of Penne in front of him, and his uncle poured him some

Chianti. "Buon appetito!" he exclaimed as he dug into the Penne.

His aunt and uncle, both tickled pink at their new house guest, sat down and began eating as well.

"Oh, this is delicious, Zia. I'm famished!"

"Thank you, Dante." She always loved when the people she cherished enjoyed her cooking.

"So, Zio, when is Riccardo coming?"

"He said he would be here tomorrow," Giuditta said excitedly. She couldn't wait to see her son. It had been months.

"So, what does he do in Cuneo?"

"He lives in Alba, which is a small city in the province of Cuneo, in Piedmont."

"He lives there with his girlfriend Raffaella. They met at work." Alberto proudly said.

"Oh, at work. Where do they work?"

"At the Ferrero factory."

"Ferrero? You mean as in Nutella? That Ferrero?"

"Oh yes, that Ferrero." Alberto took a sip of Chianti.

"Oh, I love Nutella!"

"Who doesn't?"

CHAPTER THREE

March 2020

"Go check out the view, Dante." His aunt insisted and pushed him to go out and see the view.

Dante really did not want to go out. It was cold and he was quite comfy-cozy inside, thank you very much. He moved closer to the glass. "Ah yes, Zia, it is quite a view."

"Oh, come on Dante, you cannot see everything from there. Go on, go out and look. There's a beautiful sight out there. Go. Go." She insisted.

He chose not to argue with his aunt, since he'd been there only a couple of weeks. "Fine." He tried his best not to allow his attitude to leak into his voice.

When Dante stepped onto the balcony to take in the view of Florence, he was floored by the magnificent sight! His aunt was right. He nodded his agreement with her description that it was something out of a postcard. Then his eyes wandered over to an exquisite sight: a young woman sitting on the opposite side of the balcony, with her legs up on the railing, attentively reading a book. The two apartments shared one balcony that was divided by a floor-to-ceiling partition made of perforated metal. There was a gap of several inches between the partition and its framework. The Giglio of Florence, or the Florence fleur-de-lis, was etched into the metal, directly in the center, with open space around it. Dante leaned a bit to peek through the largest opening to get a better look at the woman. His eyes widened at the sight. She had the darkest black hair he had ever seen. From his angle, he could tell she had big eyes, but from his vantage point he couldn't make out the color. Her skin was as white as snow. It seemed to him that she must never have seen the sun.

How could that be? he thought. Surely, she goes to the beach. He shrugged. Maybe she's a mountain girl. She sure is pretty. His eyes floated to her legs which, although covered with heavy leggings, were perfectly shaped. In moving closer to get a better look, he hit one of his aunt's dried out plants which toppled over. "Crap!"

She set her legs down. "Chi è?" she asked as she turned to look at Dante.

"Oh, scusa, signorina." He leaned over the balcony so she could see who he was.

She smiled warmly at him. "Ah, sei Dante vero?" she had been told by his aunt that he was coming. She had heard a lot about him. Something told her that she knew a bit too much about this man already.

"Yes…uh…si…sono Dante." He waved. "E tu chi sei?"

"My name is Serenella." She got up to shake his hand.

She wasn't wearing gloves, but her hand was warm anyway, and it radiated through his hands and all throughout his body. "Very nice to meet you. So, you speak English?"

"Not very well, I'm afraid."

"That's okay. I have to learn Italian, so you can speak Italian to me, if you're more comfortable."

"Very well." She said in Italian. "Italian it is." Again, she gave him a warm smile.

Suddenly, the chill evaporated from his body. Her friendly smile exuded warmth like a comfortable heater. "Thank you. I need to learn Italian because of the job I'm starting next week."

"Yes, your aunt told me about this new job of yours." She leaned on her balcony, just as he was. "So, tell me about it."

"Well, I work for a company called LCD which is headquartered in Canada."

"Canada? That's quite far."

"Yes, it is but it's not too far from where I live."

"And where do you live?"

"In Woodbridge, Ontario. It's just a few kilometers north of Toronto."

25

"Oh, Toronto. I heard that that it is a beautiful city. So clean. And everyone is polite."

"Oh yes, it is beautiful but not so clean as it used to be. And trust me, not everyone is polite."

"Ah, no?"

"Have you ever been there?" he wondered if he had ever seen her.

"Oh no, but my friend Tina did go there. She studied at the University of Toronto for a few years."

"Wow, what a small world. Did she like it?"

"Yes, she loved it, but she didn't want to stay there. It was too cold for her." She inched a bit closer to Dante.

"Ha ha…Oh, I can understand that. It can get pretty cold in Canada. But our area is not so bad. Try going out west in the prairie provinces. Now, that is cold."

"What are the prairie provinces?"

"They would be Manitoba, Saskatchewan, and Alberta. These three provinces are the coldest in North America, for sure. These provinces have a lot of wide-open spaces, and the wind blows through there with nothing to stop it."

"Okay, well, I don't think I'll be going there anytime soon. I don't like the cold. I was born and raised in Florence and this past January was the coldest it has ever been."

"Well, I can tell you that March in Toronto is never like this one. It's so beautiful today. Look at that view!"

She gazed out onto the Florentine landscape. "It is indeed marvelous. I've lived here all my life and this view always takes my breath away."

Giuditta gently moved the embroidered white curtains to the side so she could peek at the couple. She loved what she saw. Something had told her to give Dante a bit of a push, so to speak, to go out on the balcony and enjoy the view. And now he was enjoying Serenella's company. She turned to Alfredo, who was watching the news on TV, and gestured to him. He was so engrossed in what he was watching that he didn't notice her. Then the news anchor's story piqued her interest.

"Today, Prime Minister Giuseppe Conte declared the entire country a red zone, meaning people should stay home except for work and emergencies. The move expands the emergency measures already in place in northern Italy, which is where most of the nine thousand cases are reported. And, so far, four-hundred and sixty-three deaths."

The video cut to a clip of the prime minister saying, "This situation is very grave. I am urging all citizens of Italy to cooperate with officials and follow the restrictions in place."

The announcer continued. "The prime minister has introduced a new slogan for citizens to live by: I'm staying home. Italy is a protected zone. We will be updating our viewers as this crisis develops."

"I can't believe this!" Giuditta exclaimed.

"I am dumbfounded! We have had health issues in the past, but never like this. Oh, our poor Italy!"

Dante and Serenella were completely oblivious to the news story. They were busy creating a new friendship—and maybe even something more.

"Serenella, come inside please." Her father said.

"What is it Papà?" she did not like the look on his face.

"We can talk inside."

Bruno Torretti was not much for chit chat, especially since his wife died in 2010 from breast cancer. Serenella, seventeen at the time, stepped up to the plate and took care of her father while she studied to make something of herself. He made her want for nothing, and she had grown extremely close to him. It was just the two of them, and he hoped it would stay that way for a long time. But alas, he knew well that sooner or later, she would find a man and marry. That thought saddened him terribly.

"I'm sorry, I must go."

"Dante, can you please come inside? We must talk." Alfredo seemed rather serious. He was anxious. Dante had never seen him like this.

"Yes, Zio." He said a silent ciao to Serenella and stepped inside.

"Papà, what is going on? You're scaring me."

"You need to see this." Bruno had put the TV on pause while he called in his daughter. He pressed play and the exact same newscast that had played on Alfredo's TV, started playing on his own. Serenella's face darkened as the news seeped into her young brain.

"What does all this mean? I don't understand." She was horrified at the new regulations that were emanating from the television. "We can't go anywhere? We have to stay home? We can't go to work? We can't go shopping unless it is absolutely necessary? This is outrageous!"

"I know, Serenella, I know. This is ludicrous. Never in my life have I heard these rules coming out of Rome."

"So, what do we do, Papà?"

"I'm afraid we don't have a choice. We must comply." His mouth tightened.

"I'm calling Egidio." She picked up her phone, searched for a contact, and hit the call button. "Ciao, Egidio, did you hear the news?"

"Yes, I did." She could hear the anger in his voice. "You come to work on Monday and then we'll see. I must make some phone calls. I simply cannot close my doors— cannot! I have people depending on me for their livelihood. This cannot happen."

"Well, they did say it should only be for two weeks in order to flatten the curve."

"Still, two weeks is a long time. I will lose a lot of money!" then a chain of curse words rolled off his tongue.

"All right. Well, I will see you Monday then."

"Yes." He hung up.

~~~~~~

"What is this? What does it mean?" Dante couldn't quite grasp what the television anchor was saying.

"Well, there is a very infectious virus called Coronavirus that is spreading rapidly and is infecting many people. They are ordering a two-week quarantine for all residents and visitors, including tourists."

"But that's impossible. I have work to do. I can't stay here! I'll go nuts!" Dante looked around at the miserably sized apartment which was the size of his room at home. He panicked. He got up and began pacing.

His uncle let him go for a few minutes then stopped him. "Dante, come sit."

"No, Zio, I have to call my boss." He went to his bedroom and made a WhatsApp call to his boss. Within seconds, both men were engrossed in a video call.

"Dante! Hey dude! How are you doing? Did you get to Italy okay? How is it over there? Lots of young chicks, eh?" he was clueless.

"I'm okay, but Italy is not okay."

"What do you mean by that?"

"Well, have you heard about this Coronavirus thing?"

"Yeah, I heard something on the news. Why?"

"Well, the Italian government is quarantining us, and that includes me. They ordered us to not leave our homes for two weeks." Dante was becoming more and more agitated, as the news sunk in.

"Two weeks! That's absurd. This is only a form of the flu, from what I have heard. Here in Calgary, it's business as usual."

"Okay, so what do I do?"

"Stay put, Dante. Let me look into this." And his face disappeared from Dante's phone.

Dante was mortified. He had looked high and low, and finally found this terrific opportunity. And now, because of the Italian government, he might lose it. He shook his head and headed for the television room.

"What did your boss say?"

"He's going to look into it. He doesn't know much right now."

The next morning, Serenella was out on the balcony reading again. Dante saw her from the corner of his eye while he was eating a cornetto filled with Nutella. He hurriedly ate it and gulped down his latte, grabbed his phone, and stepped onto the balcony.

"Good morning Serenella." He tried to sound chipper.

As she turned her head to look at him, her pitch-black hair fluttered in the breeze like an ocean wave. Her dark brown eyes lit up when she saw his face. "Ciao, Dante.

Dante stayed silent for a moment, collecting his thoughts. He faced the direction of Florence which was peeking over the horizon. "I guess you heard the news…"

She nodded with a frown.

"This is crazy."

"Sure is."

They stayed on that balcony for over two hours, talking. They talked about their jobs, their families, and their friends—but not about the virus. It seemed they both wanted to erase it from their minds and thus from their lives.

On March 24, Prime Minister Giuseppe Conte appeared in a livestream press conference.

"My fellow Italians, today I announce a new decree approved by the Council of Ministers. This decree increases fines for violating the restrictions and regulations that the Parliament has declared during the emergency. It includes the possibility of reducing or suspending public and private transportation. We are also giving the regional governments power to impose additional restrictive regulations in their regions for a maximum of seven days before being confirmed as a National Decree."

"What is he saying?" Dante asked angrily.

"Basically, the government is stopping all public and private transportation, and it will be regulated by local authorities." Alfredo clarified.

"What? Why?" he was losing his temper.

"Well…he says because the virus is spreading very quickly, and they think this will slow it down."

Dante tightened his lips, shook his head, and went to his room.

CHAPTER FOUR

April 2020

Dante went out on the balcony and knocked on the metal partition in the hopes that Serenella would hear. He waited impatiently.

"I'm here." She appeared at their favorite spot.

"Oh, thank God." He took her hand and placed it on his chest. "I'm lost. I just heard that they extended the lockdown until April 13. I can't work, I can't make money, and I'm stuck here. This is outrageous!"

She felt his heart beating through his T-shirt. The next question was one she was afraid to hear the answer to, but she had to ask it. "Can you just go back home?"

"No, Canada has stopped all flights from Italy because it seems like this is the epicenter of the outbreak." He tightened his grip on her hand.

"Dante, you're hurting me."

He immediately loosened his grip. "Oh! Sorry! I'm so sorry, Serenella, I just...just..."

With her right hand, she stroked his sculptured face. "Dante, just take a deep breath. We will get through this. We are friends, no?"

"Yes," he smiled softly.

"Well, then, we must stick together."

Those words gave him intense hope and strength. "Yes, you're right." Then he smirked. "You must think I'm a weak man."

"No! no! I don't!" She felt his toxic masculinity flowing through her hand, up her arm, and wrapping around her heart. She loved that in a man. Someone who could take charge, not like some of the feminized Italian boys she knew. "You're simply scared, as I am, as we all are. I have never been in this situation, ever."

"Neither have I."

"Well, then we must be strong. And we have each other, so we can get through whatever this is."

"Serenella." He moved in closer. "Do you want to go out?"

"Out? Where? All the places are closed. We cannot go anywhere."

"Let's find a place where nobody can see us."

"Oh…I…um…Giardino Della Fortezza...that's a perfect place."

"Where is that?"

"Just a few blocks away."

"Walking distance?"

"Yes." She smiled.

"Good. Let's go."

"Now?"

"Yes. Now. Please?"

"Well, we're going to need an excuse to go out." She tapped her temple lightly. "Ah! Groceries! We are going out to buy groceries! I will see if Papà needs anything. You check with your aunt."

"Yes ma'am!" And just like that, all the worry turned into excitement. He flew inside. "Zia, I'm going to the store, do you need anything?"

"Oh, Dante, you cannot go. You know that."

"Listen, Zia. If I am buying necessities, the cops won't say anything. I have a mask…" he pulled one from his pocket. His mom mailed it to him from Canada. "Please, Zia. give me a list."

Giuditta looked at her nephew with inquisitive eyes. "Are you going alone?"

"No, I'm going with Serenella." He knew she suspected something. She always smiled at him when she noticed he was out talking with her.

"Ah, I see." She went into her junk drawer, pulled out a notepad and a pen, and wrote a few items on the small piece of paper. "Here you go." Then she pulled some money out of her apron pocket.

"No, Zia! I have this. I insist."

Giuditta shrugged and slipped the money back into the pocket. She hugged Dante. "Please be careful and keep your mask on."

"Yes, Zia." He skipped a step as he went out on the balcony, looking for his new girlfriend. He did not have to wait long.

"Here, I have a list. Do you have one?"

Dante showed her the list. She peered at it.

"That's only a few things."

"Oh, don't worry, I'll add some stuff. I always do when I go shopping." He laughed wholeheartedly.

"Very good. I'll see you downstairs."

Dante quickly went back to his room, slipped his phone into his jeans jacket pocket, slid the list inside his wallet where there was a prepaid credit card mailed to him by his parents, along with a half dozen handmade masks. He had been officially furloughed and couldn't work. He had promised his parents that he would pay back every penny once this crisis was over. He raced down the stairs, skipping as many steps as possible without falling, and ending up outside in the courtyard. No more than a few seconds passed before Serenella appeared. She had on a pair of jeans with a few tears in them, as the current style called for, a white jeans jacket, and a plain gray tee shirt that hugged her upper body, showing off her bouncy round breasts.

"You are a vision!" He took her in his arms, held her face in his hands, and slowly kissed her lips: at first brushing them, ever so lightly. Then he looked into her eyes, searching for opposition. None. He kissed her again, this time with fervor and desire, searching for her tongue. Their feverish exchange lasted but a minute, but, of course, time seems to stand still for lovers.

"What if I have the coronavirus?" she whispered very sensually into his ear. She knew well that many ears were listening in.

He shivered just a bit. Not from the words, but from the intimacy of the whisper. "I don't care," was all he could muster. He placed his arm around her shoulder and guided her to the large gateway that led to the street. They both looked around, scrutinizing the area for Municipal Police. Those were the scoundrels that were giving out citations.

"The coast is clear."

They clasped their hands together and began walking down the street towards the park, while keeping their eyes peeled for the authorities. With their masks dangling from their arms, like extra-long bracelets, they talked and joked. As they reached the park, they noticed it was cordoned off with bright yellow tape.

"Oh, shit!"

"Wait! I know another way." Serenella pulled her man in a different direction. She made extra sure there were no people around, then pulled Dante into a heavily wooded area. She found the perfect spot—right in the middle of six shade trees.

"Here, this is perfect." She pulled a small blanket from her backpack and extended it so the wind would unfurl it, like some sort of flag, as she laid it on the ground. She knelt on it.

"Yes, it is." Dante pulled some food, along with a bottle of Chianti, from his backpack.

They ate, drank, and made out. They talked some more, giggled, watched funny videos on YouTube, not noticing that someone was staring at them in silence. It was four hours later! When Serenella rolled onto her back with Dante on top of her, she gasped loudly. "Oh!" Her eyes opened wide in surprise, as they beheld a uniformed figure.

"What?" Dante followed the trajectory of Serenella's eyes. "Oh…" he straightened up.

"You know this is not allowed, right?"

They both stood up and began packing their things.

"Yes, we do, officer, but we were just trying to be together."

He was not much older than they were, and he understood their needs. But his uniform gave him the power to abruptly end their date. "I should give you a citation…" he crossed his arms, "but I won't—not this time" he pointed towards the street. "Now, please leave before I change my mind."

"Yes! Thank you, officer! Thank you!" Dante exclaimed as he hoisted his backpack onto his shoulders and walked off with his girl, arm in arm. They both waved at the officer, who responded with a furtive smile. He shook his head in amusement and went on to the next couple that was hiding out.

"Oh, that was close."

"It was."

They enjoyed what they had gotten away with. When they reached the market entrance, another Vigile Urbano was there. This one did not look anywhere nearly as accommodating. They placed themselves in the socially-distanced line and waited for their turn to enter.

"What are you two doing here?"

"We've come to shop. We need necessities." That was the magic word, now, if you wanted to go anywhere or do anything.

"Do you have masks?"

They both waved their masks in the air so the officer could clearly see them.

"Very well, put them on and go in. Are you together?"

"Yes, we are a couple." Dante confirmed.

Serenella liked to hear that. This made things official, and she couldn't have been more thrilled. They did as they were told and entered the market grabbing a sanitized shopping cart on their way in. Even the carts were small, just like everything else in Italy, Dante noticed.

The market had an abundance of food. Salami, cheeses, meats, and all sorts of tasty delicacies were arranged everywhere the eye could see. They pulled out their respective lists and began placing the items in their cart. As they passed the different aisles, they noticed that paper products were missing.

"Why is there no toilet paper or paper towels or tissues?"

"I heard they are scarce, and everyone has bought too much of them. They are now being rationed." She peered onto his list. "Why? Do you need toilet paper or something?"

"Yes, I need paper towels," he said as he came upon a sign which read:

Due to the urgent health crisis, this product is limited to one per family.

"But there's nothing here."

"Let's go ask the cashier." Serenella walked up to the register. "Excuse me, miss?"

"Yes." She sounded accommodating enough, but the expression on her face seemed to shout, "Don't disturb me!"

"Are there any paper towels?"

"I don't know. Let me check." She unhooked her walkie-talkie from her apron and squawked into it. "Marcello, vieni qui per favore?"

Seconds later, a very handsome young Italian male appeared, wearing the same apron as the cashier, and holding his walkie-talkie. "Si?" he asked.

"They have a question for you." And she proceeded to check out her next customer.

Marcello looked at Serenella with desiring eyes, as if he wanted to swallow her up. "Posso essere d'aiuto?" he asked her specifically.

Dante stood in front of Serenella with a facial expression that warned, "Don't even think about it!" "Si, vogliamo la carta da cucina, per favore."

His eyes squinted with an angry glare. Who was this guy? "Venite domani mattina alle sette in punto. Il camion arriva presto."

"Vabbè." Dante grabbed his girlfriend's hand and led her toward the register. "There's no way I'm coming here at seven for paper towels!" he smirked as he loaded the groceries on the counter.

"What if I come with you?"

"Well, that changes everything." He showed his pearly whites, even though they were hidden behind the mask. "As long as you're with me, I don't care how early it is."

"All right then, it's a date." She smiled warmly at her man.

As Dante walked in the door, he heard cheering. Good news maybe? He thought. He walked into the kitchen and set the bags down. "What's going on Zia?" he asked as he sat in front of the TV.

"We have a spark of hope."

"The Prime Minister announced to a starter plan for Phase Two that is to begin on May 4th. Movements across regional lines will still be forbidden, but travel between municipalities would be allowed only for work and health reasons, as well as for visits to relatives. The plan will allow re-opening of manufacturing industries and construction sites, but for now schools, bars, restaurants, and hairdressers and other "non-essential" locations will remain closed." The news anchor moved on to other news.

With a glimmer of hope of returning to work, Dante called his boss again.

"Hey Dante. How's it going over there?"

"Oh, not so good. A lot of dead people, man."

"I heard it's mainly in the north. Is that true?"

"Yeah, mainly in Lombardy, Veneto and Piedmont."

"Wow, that's some scary shit."

"Sure is."

"What's up?"

"Do you have any news on my job? Any changes?"

"I haven't heard anything from our Italian manufacturers but let me call them, okay?"

"Yeah, sure. I'll wait. Nothing else to do…ha ha…"

"Hang in there, buddy."

"Yeah, I will."

CHAPTER FIVE

May 2020

The ringtone from his cell phone jarred Dante out of his reverie. It was another WhatsApp video call.

"Ciao Dante. How are you doing?" Riccardo asked.

"I'm okay. Trying to survive...you know," smiling at the camera.

"Oh yes, I know well. Our factory finally opened and we're back at work. You know, we cannot live without Nutella. I guess we're an essential business! Ha-ha!"

"Oh man, you aren't kidding!"

"So, when are you coming to visit?"

"I don't know if I can."

"Let me find out and I'll get back with you."

"Sounds good. So, let me ask you..."

"What?"

"If I come up, can you take me on a tour of your factory?"

"It's not mine but I think I can...I'll have to make sure though...you know how it is."

"Yes, I do." Dante passed the phone to his aunt.

"Ciao Ricky, come stai?"

"I'm good Mamma. We're finally back at work up here."

"Yes, I'm so glad to hear that." She blew her son a kiss. "I miss you so very much."

"I know mamma, I know. Don't worry, I'll come down as soon as I'm permitted."

"All right, my son, I will see you soon."

"Yes mamma. Be strong and know that I love you."

"I know you do. Grazie amore!"

Riccardo's handsome face disappeared from Dante's phone. "Here you are." She handed the phone back to Dante.

"Thank you, Zia." He kissed her on the cheek for encouragement. He had been noticing the toll that this pandemic was taking on her. He couldn't wait for all this to be over. He was torn between returning to Canada to his family and friends, and continuing his relationship with Serenella. He had grown to love her, and she was a rock for him during the entire ordeal. When she said those three magic words, it cemented their relationship. He even introduced her, via WhatsApp video, to his parents and sisters. They were all happy for Dante, except his mother. Sofia was not dealing well with this forced distance between her and her favorite child. It was killing her. And now this girl! That was too much.

Santo texted his son:

Dante, please don't show your girlfriend to your mom, okay?

Why, dad?

It's too much for her. She's dealing with you being stuck in Italy. She doesn't know when you'll return. She can't come to visit. Her business is not doing well. It's just too much, son.

I understand but I'm dealing with my own shit, dad. I'm living in this tiny apartment with Zio and Zia. They're terrific but man it's tight here. I'm still not working. The only person who is getting me through this crap is Serenella. If it weren't for her, I'd probably be in the Arno river by now.

I get it. Thank God the housing market is still strong because I wouldn't know what to do with myself. Then I come home to your mom who's a pain in my neck. I have to live with her! So please, do me a favour. Just chat with your mom alone and don't mention your girlfriend, okay?

Fine!

Thanks for understanding Dante.

Dante was upset with his father, but he did see how his mom was suffering. She was pale and had lost a lot of weight. He was really worried about her. He even begged his sisters to be more supportive. Both countries were going through an extremely tough time. Italians and Canadians alike were glued to their televisions to get updated changes of rules and regulations, which seemed to change daily, with small glimmers of hope here and there.

"Dante, Serenella is asking for you." Giuditta yelled into the hallway.

"Coming!" he quickly made his way to the balcony.

"Here I am."

Serenella was holding two cocktail glasses with some red liquid. "Here, I made these for us."

Dante took his glass. "What is this?"

"Alchemies of Florence." She proudly announced.

He looked at it attentively. "And what's in it?"

"A number of things…oh…just take a sip…"

"Okay, here goes." He took a quick sip. "Mmmmm, this is good." Then he took a larger sip. "Yes, really good!"

"Glad you like it." She took a sip, herself.

"So, what's the occasion?" he took another sip.

"Our union. It has been three months since we've met, right here on this balcony."

Dante smiled from ear to ear. "Yes, it has. I've been so wrapped up in this stupid situation that I missed it. I'm sorry, love." He kissed her passionately.

"So, I was wondering…" she smacked her lips after she took another sip. "Would you like to come over for dinner?"

"And celebrate? Yes, of course."

"Oh, wonderful!" She clapped her hands joyously as she jumped up and down. "Seven sharp! Don't be late!" and she disappeared into her kitchen.

Dante took a quick trip out to the infamous market where they had shopped a while ago. He could not go away empty handed, so he bought a bouquet of flowers for his belle and a bottle of Tuscan wine for her father. At seven sharp he knocked on Serenella's door. As if she was waiting for him, she opened the door and smiled. *How handsome he is! I hope papà likes him too.*

"Come." She pulled him in as he extended his right hand holding the bouquet. "Oh, beautiful! Are they for me?"

"Yes." He held out his other hand holding the wine, "and this is for your dad."

After being in Italy for three months, he had mastered the language rather well. He wasn't fluent yet, but his young mind would reach that goal eventually.

"Buona sera, Dante." Bruno extended his hand, awaiting a shake.

"Buona sera, Signor Torretti." He placed the wine on the table and shook Bruno's hand firmly.

Good handshake. Bruno was pleased. "Please call me Bruno."

"Very well, Bruno, it's very nice to meet you."

Dante sat. "So, what's for dinner?"

51

"Pappa di Pomodoro and Arista Alla Fiorentina with a surprise for dessert."

"Mmmmm, can't wait."

The two men made themselves comfortable as Serenella began to dish out the Pappa.

"Smells delicious. What is this? Smells like a tomato soup."

"Yes, it is a tomato soup. But Tuscany style."

"Yes, Serenella inherited her mother's culinary skills. She is an excellent cook." He gulped a spoonful. "You've outdone yourself, my daughter."

"Thank you Papà." She sat and began eating the pappa too.

"So, Dante, tell me your intentions."

Dante nearly choked on his food. Then he looked up at Bruno.

"Papà, now is not the time. Please." She got up and went to Dante to pat him on his back.

"No...no...no...I'm okay. really..." he mustered between coughing fits.

Bruno was amused but tried to keep a stern look on his face. He continued to eat while his daughter tended to her boyfriend.

After several minutes of silence Dante said, out of nowhere, "Good."

"What? The soup?" Serenella asked.

"No…I mean yes…the soup is perfect, but I was answering your father."

"Oh, good intentions you mean?"

"Yes, Bruno, that's exactly what I mean. My intentions are good."

Serenella could cut the tension in the air with a knife. So, she decided to remove the soup dishes and serve the roast with the salad and the small roasted potatoes she had prepared. She did not utter a word during the preparation. She, too, was curious as to how Dante would answer her father's next question. She knew well there were going to be more.

"So, tell me, Dante, what will you do when you return to America?"

"Canada."

"Canada. America. Same thing." He shrugged, waving him off and took a bite out of the roast.

"Well, actually, they are two different countries—but that's okay." It really rankled him that every Italian seemed to think that Canada and America were the same country. He was weary of explaining it.

"You didn't answer my question. What will you do when you return to your country? What then?"

"I don't know. I haven't thought about it."

Serenella was disappointed when her father looked at her with raised eyebrows. She read them well. I told you so.

"Can we please change the subject?" She was becoming quite uncomfortable, now.

"Yes, let's," her father said with a smirk.

"I'll bet you can't wait to start working." She looked in Dante's direction.

"You got that right. I will have to take precautions, but I'm okay with them. As long as I can start earning money."

"How long will you be staying in Italy?" Bruno asked.

That was a good question. The pandemic already had taken three months away from his assignment and he wasn't sure what the original timeframe was. He would have to call Guy and find out. But not now.

"For a few months at least. The shutdown took away three months from my stay, so I suspect about six or so."

"What do you do, exactly?" Bruno asked.

"Well, I am a leather distributor for a company in Canada called LCD and I'm looking to sell our leather goods to factories in Italy. Since my uncle lives next door, my boss thought to start me off in Florence, and here I am." He smiled proudly.

"Ah, and which factory will you be selling your goods to?"

Dante pulled out his phone. He couldn't remember the names. He went into his contacts. "Ummm Maroni and Castellone."

Bruno laughed out loud. "Oh, that's going to be fun for you." He continued laughing.

"Why?"

"Well, both factories have been feuding for over two hundred years, and you might just initiate their world war three! Hahaha!"

Serenella explained thoroughly what her father had hinted at. She also informed him that Egidio Maroni was her boss.

"Oh, boy!" was all he could say.

"Oh yes, you're in for a good fight, I'd say."

"Okay, let's have espresso and biscotti."

"Agreed." Dante was wondering what he had gotten himself into.

CHAPTER SIX

June 2020

"Let's go to the beach!" Serenella exclaimed as soon as Dante stepped out onto the balcony.

"Can we?" Dante was questioning everything now. Where could they go? When could they go? How can they get there? Every day brought new questions, because every day the rules changed. Wear a mask. Don't wear a mask Take the bus. Don't take the bus. Take the train. Line up. Stay two meters apart. No need to stay apart. This was agonizing, to say the least!

"Yes, we can. The nearest beach is Viareggio but let me check to see if they are open." Serenella pulled out her phone and asked, "Siri, can you tell me if Viareggio Beach is open to the public?"

The soft-spoken computerized voice of Siri replied, "Viareggio Beach is now open to the public."

"Bravo! Bravo!" they both shouted simultaneously.

"I'll get my bathing suit and meet you downstairs." She was looking forward to the beach after all this time being locked down and treated like a prisoner. She needed a change of pace.

"Oh, wait! I don't have a bathing suit."

"Oh, can you borrow one from your uncle?"

"Oh, right…let me see…" he took off inside. "Zia, do you know if Zio has an extra bathing suit?"

"Yes, I believe so, why?"

"Serenella and I are going to the beach and I don't have a suit."

Giuditta broke a hidden smile and disappeared into her bedroom. A few minutes later she handed over a dark blue pair of swimming trunks to Dante.

"Thank you, Zia!" he hugged her and went to his room skipping a few steps along the way.

She smiled and shook her head. He's a goner.

"There you are." Serenella was happily loading her yellow FIAT 500 with beach paraphernalia.

"Need a hand?"

"No, I got this." She waved him off. "Go on get in."

Dante hesitated. He wondered how he was going to fit in such a tiny car.

"What? Do you want to drive?"

"Ummm…no…I don't know how I'm going to fit in this thing."

"What are you saying? Much bigger men have driven this car."

Dante looked at the car again, shrugged his shoulders, and opened the passenger door. He sat in the seat. "Um…okay…this might work."

"Oh, you'll be fine." She got in and cranked the engine. "Let's go!" she put the car into first gear and took off.

"Wow, this thing has spunk."

"Yes, it is Italian after all."

"Actually, it's a Chrysler."

"No way, we've had the 500 for more than sixty years."

"I'm telling you, it's a Chrysler." He pulled his phone out and Googled FIAT Chrysler. "Okay, here goes…Wikipedia says that on January 29, 2014 FIAT announced a reorganization and intended merger into a new holding company. FIAT S.p.A. and Chrysler Group LLC merged into FCA on October 12, 2014 following approval of the board on June 15, 2014 and shareholders on August 1, 2014. So, there."

"Well, what do you know? I was wrong."

"Can you repeat that for the microphone please?" he held an imaginary microphone in front of her face.

"Never!" she laughed wholeheartedly.

They were quiet during the remaining hour or so drive. The Tuscany landscape is a beautiful blend of gently rolling hills leading on to sharply peaked mountains that grow a variety of crops from vines to wheat to corn to alfalfa. The many shades of green were plentiful, as were the small lakes and rivers.

Finally, over the horizon, a body of sparkling blue water appeared!

"Ah, we're here!" Dante moved forward to get a better view.

"Yes, only a few minutes now." Serenella was thrilled to see the sea. She had not been there since the previous summer.

"It's breathtaking!"

"Oh yes, our part of the sea is one of the cleanest in Italy."

"You know what? As long as we don't get this stupid virus, I'm done with this lockdown. I want freedom."

About a half hour later, the couple was lying on the beach, facing the clear blue water, stomachs down, hands locked together, exchanging kisses.

"Now, this is much better."

"Oh yes! No partition between us!"

"I'm really glad I met you on the balcony."

"Why do you say that Dante?"

"Well, if it weren't for you, I wouldn't have been able to get through all this."

"Really?"

"Oh yes, I would have probably pulled my hair out of my head and have a bunch of bruises on my forehead from slamming my head against the wall every day."

"Oh, come now, it's not that bad."

"Yes, it is. BUT. It's been much easier with you around." His lips brushed hers, ever so softly. "I love you, Serenella." There it was. Right out in the open, now.

She was stunned but her heart fluttered at the declaration of this sweet and handsome man. "I love you too, Dante." She kissed him back.

Thank God, he thought. But then a bad thought popped into his head. Mom! How will she react?

She got up and pulled him up too. "Come on, let's go for a swim."

That negative thought evaporated as he followed her into the water, both of them making quite a splash with their feet.

~~~~~~

"What do you mean, out on a date?" Sofia asked.

"He went to the beach with Serenella. She's our neighbor's daughter."

Sofia was incredulous. "How could Dante be interested in some girl he barely knew? That was insane. He's supposed to be working, not dating."

"Oh, come on Sofia! They're young and in love—"

"In love?" Sofia was having none of it! There is no way she would allow her only son to date some floozy she didn't approve of. "What makes you think they are in love?"

Giuditta knew Sofia very well, even though they lived on two separate continents divided by a vast watery expanse. When they chatted over WhatsApp, Sofia would go on and on about her precious Dante. Dante this. Dante that. Brag, brag, brag. But, as Giuditta came to know Dante, she realized he was trying to extricate himself from his mother's clenches. And now she was having a great time shoving this new reality in Sofia's face. "Sofia, I don't think Dante needs your approval. He is twenty-nine years old. He is a grown man and he seems quite mature enough to make his own decisions on his love life. Frankly, I think you should butt out."

Immediately, the screen went blank.

Well, I guess she didn't like that truth. "Mamma mia!" she exclaimed as she closed the cover on her iPad. "Time for espresso!"

"Mannaggia a te!" Sofia shouted to the blank computer screen. She picked up her phone and started a video call with Dante, but it rang and rang and rang. "Well shit!"

She had been particularly worried about Dante being in Italy during the lockdown. She did everything she could to get him to come home but he refused. She wondered why he would never answer her and now she knew why. Even though Santo, Gianna and AnnaBella had tried to convince her that Dante was indeed old enough to make his own decisions on life, she pushed back. She had to find another way to have her son return to Canada as soon as possible. But how?

~~~~~~

"Hey, I just got a text from my boss."

"Oh, and what is he saying?"

Hey Dante, I've received the okay for you to begin your assignment. Are you still available?

"Well, that's good news. What are you going to say?"

He punched in some characters using both thumbs.

Of course, I'm available.

Perfect! I'll email you the details shortly.

He showed the text to Serenella. "Man, I can't wait to start!"

"Oh, Dante, I'm so happy for you."

She parked her car in the small garage and turned the engine off. "I have to tell you something."

"Oh, and what is it?" he helped her empty the car.

"I work for Maroni Leather Works."

"You do?"

"Yes, ever since I finished school."

"Wow! What a small world."

"Yes, but there's more."

"There is?"

"Remember we talked about the feud between the Castellone Leather Company and Maroni that's been going on for over two hundred years?"

"Yes, a feud. You mean like between Romeo Montague and Juliet Capulet?

"Yes, exactly."

"So, what does this mean for me?"

They reached the top of the stairs.

"It means they are going to start another feud to win your leather hides."

"Oh, I see." He helped to bring her stuff inside her apartment. "Yes, I do see where there could be a problem."

"Ciao Papà!" she shouted.

"Hello Bruno!" he didn't want to be rude.

"So, what do you suggest?"

"I think you should act like you don't know me and make an unbiased decision."

"Did anyone ever tell you how smart you are?" he quickly kissed her and left. He didn't want to get caught by her father. Bruno caught the kiss from the corner of his eye and turned the other way. He liked Dante and secretly approved of his daughter's relationship with this young man. He only hoped he could make a decent living.

"Ciao Zia! I have news!" he cried as he scurried over to the kitchen.

Giuditta was taking her biscotti out of the oven. "Good news I hope."

"Oh, something smells delicious."

"Come, sit. I made espresso."

He didn't have to be told twice. He loved espresso and he especially had grown to love his aunt's biscotti. He picked one up from the steaming tray, blew on it and took a bite. "MMMMMM, Zia these are fabulous!"

"Grazie Dante!" she prepared the espresso pot. "Now, tell me the news."

"I'm finally starting work."

"That's wonderful! And when are you starting?"

"I assume within the next few days. Guy is sending me an email with all the details."

Giuditta got up to remove the espresso from the heat and poured it into two espresso cups. She placed one in front of Dante and one in front of herself. "That's good news but I know a person who is not going to take this well."

"Mamma." He frowned. "Yes, she tried to video call me, but I was at the beach. Honestly, I didn't want my day spoiled."

"Dante, she worries about you."

"I know, Zia. Too much though."

"I know but give her time. She needs to learn that you are a man and that you have your own life." She dunked a biscotto into her espresso.

Dante did the same. "I know, but it's so frustrating though. I can't shake her. I hate to say this but she's the main reason I took this job. She's like a Kraken sometimes, geez!"

Giuditta sighed. She took a sip of her espresso. "Well, she probably called you right after she chatted with me."

"Oh, really?"

"Yes, and when I told her you were old enough to make your own decisions about your life, she hung up on me."

Dante shook his head. "You know Zia, I love my mom, I really do. But she just doesn't want to let go. I don't know what to do."

Giuditta patted his hand. "Not to worry, nephew. Just live your life and let me and Zio worry about your mother." She gave him another biscotto. "Now, eat!

CHAPTER SEVEN

July 2020

"Wow, this place is amazing."

"Thank you, Dante. We are extremely proud of the work we do. We've been in this business for over two hundred years and we've always had the best quality leathers."

Dante looked over Egidio's shoulders searching for Serenella. She was waving at him from the leather jacket section.

"Ah…and here we have Serenella Torretti…" he motioned her to join them.

Serenella did not have to be told twice. Wearing a huge smile, she breezed over to where the two men were standing. Egidio looked at her, and then at Dante. Then it stuck him. "You two know each other!"

"Actually, yes we do." She looked at Dante with loving eyes. "Ciao Dante."

"Ciao Serenella." He adored her—especially when she was arrayed so professionally, wearing a suit, and her hair pulled up tight in a bun. She looked powerful, like nothing could stop her. "My uncle lives right next door to her, and we got to know each other during the lockdown."

Egidio was already seeing a great advantage he had on Castellone. This will be a cinch! LCD certainly will give me an exclusive contract! He rubbed his hands together, eagerly, like the villain with the evil plan to take over the world, in one of those old cartoons. "Well, isn't it a small world?"

"Sure is."

"Come, let me show you the rest of our store. Serenella, please join us."

He continued to walk through the facility with Dante and Serenella behind him. The young lovers subtly touched each other as much as they could. The group went through the four levels of the store where everything from wallets to shoes were displayed for sale. Then they walked up to a heavy, steel door with a sign that read, ENTRATA DIPENDENTI, or EMPLOYEES ONLY. Egidio pulled a card out of his pocket and held it to a small box on the wall next to the door. There was a loud CLICK! and buzz, and then the door opened into the workshop where all the goods they had just seen were being handcrafted. Dante took notes at every stop. He would send them to Guy at the end of his day. As he took out his phone to shoot some pictures, Egidio said, "Please! My friend! No photography is allowed in here!"

Dante replied, "I understand, Signor Maroni, but I must provide my company with some photos, so they know how their leather will be processed. I promise, I will be prudent. I'm going to send these over WhatsApp, which uses end-to-end encryption. It's more secure than email." And I've already signed your nondisclosure agreement.

Egidio shrugged his shoulders. "Very well, then. I will have to trust you."

"Thank you very much, sir."

Around one, Dante's stomach started to growl.

As if on cue, Egidio said: "So, it's one. Who's hungry?"

Both the lovebirds raised their hands, and in unison—almost in harmony—they said, "I am!" They turned to each other and giggled.

Egidio laughed. "All right then, time for lunch."

"Yes, good idea. I'll be back around two." As Dante turned, Egidio stopped him.

"Oh, no. You are not going alone. Today it is my treat. Come." He motioned them towards the door. "Serenella, go ahead and go to the Trattoria Prato Verde with Dante. I'll be there shortly."

"Okay, I'll see you there." She hooked her arm into Dante's. "Come. You will love Prato Verde. Their food is exquisite."

As they walked out of Maroni Leather Works, Mario Castellone and his daughter Evangelica were watching from their window, from which they had a perfect view of the Maronis' comings and goings.

"Look at that!" Mario was irritated. "Is that the new supplier from Canada? What the hell is Serenella doing? Is Egidio plotting against us?" his fists tightened, and he gritted his teeth in anger.

"Papi, don't worry. I have a plan." Evangelica was a drop-dead gorgeous blonde, and she knew it well. She knew that young man from Canada would fall under her spell quickly and permanently, never to re-emerge. "Let me work on him. I'll get him on our side in no time." She flashed an evil grin.

Her father ran his open hand over her long, bleach-blonde hair. "Ah, mia cara, you are devious."

"I know," she said with a giggle and a shrug. She turned on her stilettos and headed for the exit.

"I'm so proud of that girl." He was already imagining the profits he would make with the highest quality leather in the world.

~~~~~~

"Ah, you're already eating the antipasto, I see."

"Yes, we even left you some." It was obvious that Serenella had a good relationship with her boss.

Egidio pulled the chair out for his wife and waited for her to sit. "Mia cara." He gently kissed her on the cheek.

"Dante, this is my wife, Lorena." He took his seat.

"Ciao, Dante, so very nice to meet you."

The headwaiter came up to their table. "Buon pomeriggio, my name is Sergio Modena, and I will be serving you today. Volete del vino?"

"Yes, please bring us your house Chianti."

"Right away." And he left swiftly.

"So, Dante, when did you arrive in Florence?"

"I've been here since before the lockdown."

"His uncle lives next door to Serenella, Egidio added. What a pleasant surprise that was."

"Oh, what a coincidence."

"Indeed. Perhaps this time we may get the best product, instead of that stinker Mario."

Lorena patted her husband's hand. "Come now, Egidio, we've always had better products than Castellone. Their products can't hold a candle to ours."

Dante thought it poor form for them to criticize their competitor in front of him. He decided to set things straight. "Actually, I was sent here to analyze both your facilities and finished goods. Ultimately, it will be my boss, Guy Marchetti who will make the final decision. I'm simply the messenger."

"Well, Dante, I truly appreciate your honesty. You can analyze all you want because we are convinced that our products are the best in Florence. We are sure of it."

The waiter returned with the wine. He placed it on the table and took out his order pad and pen. "Now, what can I get you today?"

Egidio knew that anything they were going to eat would be exquisite. "What do you suggest, Sergio?"

Sergio straightened his back and announced: "We have Bistecca alla Fiorentina, Gnudi, Insalada di Farro and for dessert, Apple Torta."

"Sounds delicious. Bring us all of them."

"Excellent choice, signore." And once again he took off towards the kitchen.

"I must say, this place is beautiful." Dante was admiring the quaint, rustic architecture with wood-trimmed arches and whitewash paint covering the antique walls. Every arch had a painting that seemed to be from the same artist. "And these paintings are magnificent."

"Oh, yes, she is a local artist."

"That's true. Many artists in Florence are descendants of the most famous Florentine artists, but since names do not bring you fortune you must prove yourself. You know, you can find many artists on Ponte Vecchio." Serenella explained.

"Oh wow."

"Yes, and I believe there is a young man that hangs out there, and it is said that he is the direct descendant of Botticelli."

"Botticelli? I don't remember studying about him."

Egidio shook his head. These Americans have no culture. He thought. So, he pulled his phone out and did a search on Botticelli. He gave his phone to Dante.

"Sandro Botticelli was born in Florence on May 17, 1510. Oh, he painted the Birth of Venus. Oh, I know who he is. He's quite famous." He kept on reading. "Oh, how curious, he painted a self-portrait in his Adoration of the Magi and was summoned by Pope Sixtus IV to paint frescos in the Sistine Chapel. Amazing. That's a place I want to see before I leave Italy." He handed the phone back to Egidio.

Serenella felt sad at the thought of Dante leaving Italy and returning to Canada. She did not want to think about that. Not right now.

The food arrived and was served. They ate, drank, and chatted loudly—just as almost all Florentines do.

"I ate so much. I need to take a long walk," Dante exclaimed as he exited the restaurant.

"Serenella, why don't you show Dante around. Be his tour guide. This way you can kill two birds with one stone. Just don't forget to wear your masks."

The young couple rolled their eyes. How long before things could go back to normal? They were both tired of this virus.

"Yes, Egidio, thank you. I'll return in a few hours."

"No, no, Serenella. Please go home. I will see you tomorrow at eight."

Serenella transformed into tour guide mode. "Well, our beautiful city has no equal. You can scour the Italian peninsula and you won't find anywhere quite like it."

"I can't wait to see it all."

"We won't have time for everything, but we can certainly see the most important places."

"I'm good. Let's do this."

"Here is the Basilica di San Lorenzo, built by the Medici family in 393. There is a multitude of stories connected with this church. It was the Medici family's parish church. Donatello, the artist is buried here, as is Cosimo di Medici. The library Biblioteca Laurenziana is here, with a design by Michelangelo. It contains over 3,000 manuscripts!"

Dante was thoroughly impressed, not only with the historical aspect, but with Serenella's knowledge. "Wow, that's an extremely impressive history! That's what I love about Italy; everything has so much history behind it! And you would make a fabulous tour guide!"

Serenella blushed a bit, and managed a soft, "Thank you."

Serenella took him to all the places she could in the time they had. They visited the Da Vinci Museum where they experimented with interactive displays and embarked on a journey into Da Vinci's master mind with various models that demonstrate the study of gravity, mechanics, and design.

After that they visited the Galleria Dell'Accademia where the seventeen foot tall Statue of David stood depicting the moment just before his battle with Goliath. They weren't the only visitors in the gallery, and even with the strict social distancing rule, the "oohs" and "ahhs" were resounding abundantly in the hallway where Michelangelo's masterpiece stood.

The Uffizi Gallery was next. Dante was able to see Botticelli's Birth of Venus in person, along with the first painting of Michelangelo, the Holy Family with St. John the Baptist. They also viewed various paintings and sculptures of Correggio, Raphael, Caravaggio, and, of course, Leonardo Da Vinci.

Toward the end of the day, they headed to Piazza Santa Croce and entered the basilica which carried the same name. It is the largest Franciscan church in Florence. The original structure was built in 1212, when St. Francis of Assisi first visited Florence. Beyond the tri-colored marble, the church has sixteen chapels and the temple of the Italian Glories which is the resting place of Michelangelo, Galileo and Machiavelli.

They ended the tour with a classic Italian gelato that they enjoyed while sitting on a marble bench facing the basilica.

"Talk about a long walk," Dante said as he savored his delectable coffee and chocolate gelato.

"Oh yes. Even if we did have to wear a mask through everything, it was worth it."

"And this gelato tops the afternoon off in a picture-perfect way."

"It does." She took a lick of her vanilla and pistachio gelato, while looking at him seductively.

"I love this city. I can see myself living here."

Serenella's eyes lit up with hope. "Really?"

"Sure, why not?"

"I thought you'd want to return home after your work is done here."

"Well, I guess I'll have to; but if this works out for me, I'll be traveling all over the world. My company will not only be selling to Florentine factories, but factories in many countries that make leather goods—like Brazil, India, Korea, Mexico, the United States, and even Russia."

She didn't know what to make of his statement. "I suppose you won't be settling down?"

"I may…one day…but not right now. I am looking forward to traveling and working. That's what I signed up for."

After that definitive statement, Serenella had nothing to say. It was quite clear what his plans were. And she was not part of them.

After they threw the end of their cones to the few pigeons patiently waiting at their feet, Dante got up. "Do you want to go home together?" he extended his hand for hers.

She didn't give it to him. "No, I have some errands to run. I'll see you later. Okay?" she picked up her handbag and turned to walk away from him, not showing him the tears streaming down her cheeks.

Dante shrugged his shoulders and headed for the bus stop. He thought that she seemed a bit aloof—but then he noticed a pastry shop. "I'm going to bring home some pastries for Zia and Zio. They've been super great to me." He walked into the 'Pasticceria Santa Maria' and ordered a tray of the most delectable pastries showcased.

When he walked out of the pastry shop holding the pink box of pastries, he noticed a gorgeous blonde with the longest legs he'd ever seen. She was strutting proudly, carrying a Castellone original handbag with matching stilettos and a rather short fuchsia leather skirt. She was at the receiving end of whistles and growls from all the men whose heads she turned as she slowly strutted past. But she only acknowledged one man, with a coy smile and a seductive wave of her fingers: Dante.

CHAPTER EIGHT

August 2020

"Dante Fogli, nice to meet you." He extended his hand to the beautiful blonde that had waved to him about a week ago. Even though she was wearing a mask now, he could still see her chestnut eyes staring at him. He couldn't tell whether or not she was smiling under the mask.

"Your Italian is very good. I'm impressed," she remarked with an incredibly sensual voice. "My name is Evangelica Castellone, so very nice to meet you as well." She said in British English.

"Well, I'd have to say the same for your English. It's quite remarkable."

"Come Dante, let me give you a tour." Mario Castellone turned, winked at his daughter, and began the guided tour.

Evangelica hooked her arm into Dante's and asked; "I hope you don't mind?"

Dante felt uncomfortable in that situation, but he couldn't possibly refuse this gorgeous woman's flirts. How could he?

As Mario guided them through the various departments, Dante scrutinized various pieces of shoes, handbags, belts, wallets, and jackets, and by the end of the tour had determined that the quality of the Castellone products was considerably inferior to the Maroni ones. He recalled the comments of Egidio, and frankly, could not find any disagreement with them. However, he kept his comments to himself. He simply took photos of the items he looked at and sent them to Guy. He would provide his findings upon his return to Canada.

Evangelica knew exactly where Serenella had taken Dante when they left together that afternoon in July. She had one of her subordinates follow them around. She would not bring him to those boring museums and churches. No way. She wanted to offer Dante the best of Florence's night life, and maybe even seduce him along the way. She really liked Dante, enough to become his. I would look much better by his side than that simpleton Serenella, she thought. She knew where his job would take him and the thought that she could be by his side jet-setting across the globe excited her tremendously.

"Cara, why don't you show Dante the fantastic night life we have here in Florence?"

"I'd love to, Papi." She turned to Dante, "What do you say, Dante? Are you interested?"

He had to ponder that a bit. He hadn't been seeing much of Serenella lately. For some strange reason, she had turned cold. Her answers were short and curt. She seemingly had lost interest in him. Did she not love me anymore? Did she ever love me? "Yes, that sounds great."

"Perfect! Let me change clothes. I will meet you down at the entrance in about thirty minutes. All right?"

"Yes, of course." Dante shook Mario's hand and left the store. He wanted to send the photos he took to Guy. He got out into the piazza and headed for the nearest espresso shop. "Un espresso, per favore." He looked for a spot in the corner and removed his mask. He video-dialed Guy.

"Oh, hey Dante. How are things?"

"Hey Guy, yeah, things are good. Still wearing masks, still social distancing. How about over there?"

"Yeah, the same. I'm getting tired of this crap. It's so ridiculous. Small stores are closed, and these people have lost everything, whereas the big box stores are making millions. I don't understand it for the life of me. Why is it that the big guys can stay open and the little guys can't when all their customers need to do is wear a mask and social distance? This is insane."

"I agree. Here, at least, all the stores are open with precautions, but bars, stores, restaurants, museums, cinemas are all open. I don't know… this is still so surreal to me."

"Yeah. Anyway, let's talk shop. Tell me what you think of Castellone."

"Well, did you see the photos I took?"

"Yeah, not in detail but I did see them."

"What you need to do is compare them to the Maroni pix. There's a big difference in my opinion. The Maroni goods are made with great care and precision, and they use the best quality in their accessories. Honestly, I don't see LCD being a good fit with Castellone." Dante never told his boss about Serenella thinking that their relationship might cloud his judgment, but there was nothing cloudy about the Maroni goods. They were exceptional.

"Okay, Dante, send me all the info and I'll review it thoroughly."

"Will do. Gotta go. It's almost dinnertime here."

"All right, see ya man."

And the video ended.

~~~~~~

"Wow! You look amazing!"

Evangelica was wearing a silver, sparkly long spaghetti-strap dress with a side slit that revealed her long legs. "Molte grazie!" she opened her matching clutch, pulled out her car key, and headed for the midnight blue Lamborghini parked just a few steps away.

"Holy mackerel! A hot car for a hot lady!"

She simply touched the car's invisible handle and both doors flew open like an eagle showing off its wings.

"Ferrari doesn't have these," she said as she entered the driver's seat.

"Never seen one that does." He did the same. "So, where are we going?"

"To Full Up Club." She revved the engine and blasted off.

Neither of them noticed Serenella watching them from the west window that had the perfect view of the street below. She frowned and went back to her customers. *Well, I guess that is that.*

"What's that?" Dante asked.

"A dance club. Don't you have them in Canada?"

"Oh yeah, Toronto is loaded with them. I don't know if any of them are open right now, though."

"Che peccato." She was whizzing through the city like she owned it.

"Don't you ever get stopped by the cops?"

"No-pfft!" she said.

"Lucky," was all he could muster while hanging onto the grab handle.

He only had to endure her driving for twenty minutes.

"Here we are." She parked in front of a club with a large neon sign displaying, "Full Up Club". She got out and handed the fob to the valet.

"Nice." Dante got out and hurried to open the entrance door for the hot blonde. He liked this girl and he especially liked the looks of envy he got from the Italian men who would certainly kill to have her. He cocked his head up and threw out his pectorals. I could get used to this.

As soon as she entered, a dozen people began to attend to her every desire. She was greeted by men and women alike, all of whom double kissed her. The couple was escorted to a cozy seating area in the back where the music wasn't as loud. A waiter handed her what looked like a Martini.

Dante noticed that nobody in the club was wearing a mask, which he found quite refreshing. He also noticed that both the men and women were some of the most beautiful people he had ever seen. Oh, yeah, Italians know how to party. Since he was Evangelica's "plus one," he got the royal treatment right along with her.

"What do you drink?" a stunning brunette asked.

"Ummm…a Peroni I guess."

"Coming right up."

"So, Dante, what do you think?"

"This is dope, as we say back home."

"Dope? I thought that meant drugs."

"Well, it does, but it's the feeling you get when you take drugs, get it?"

"Yes, I understand." She snapped her fingers. "Speaking of which." She showed him a mirrored tray containing all sorts of substances that certainly were illegal in both countries. She raised her eyebrows giving him an inquisitive look.

"What's this?"

"Oh, come now! Don't you know what this is?"

He looked the drugs over and shook his head. "I'll pass." Somehow his dad's voice popped into his head. "Don't take that shit, Dante! It will ruin your life! Trust me."

"What? Come on Dante, where's your sense of adventure?"

"Not with this stuff."

She waved the goodie tray away. "So, are you hungry at least?"

"Yes, that I am."

"Okay, let's go then." She got up and headed to the dining room where another group of people attended to her. "Sit."

Dante pulled a chair out for her, and after she was seated, he sat in his own chair.

"Oh, chivalry? I thought it was lost."

"Not with me." He smiled. Some young guy brought him his beer poured into a glass. When he noticed that he winked at Evangelica, he knew something was up. He casually slid it to the side, never taking a sip from it.

Some food was set on the table, along with some wine. He noticed no exchanges of secret looks or winks or blinks of any sort, so he enjoyed the food. He was famished, but he didn't want the wine, so he asked for a Fanta in a can. He did not want to drink anything that wasn't opened right in front of him. His gut told him not to trust Evangelica. She seemed to him to be like a devil in disguise. He had never fallen for this kind of woman, and he was not about to now.

"Come on, let's dance." She pulled him onto the dance floor. He was a bit stiff at first, but then he started to warm up. The Italian dance music pounded in the highest of decibels, but that didn't seem to bother anyone on the floor. Rather, it made them turn and spin faster and wilder as the night went on. As the night dragged on, Dante grew more and more disenchanted.

When they returned to their seats at the table, Dante ordered a San Pellegrino Chinotto—again in a can. When it arrived he gulped it down like plain water. "This is terrific." He crushed the can once the liquid was drained. He began to notice that his "date" wasn't very pleased with him. Ha!

Gotcha! he thought as he showed her his pearly whites. "Another Chinotto please!"

Before it arrived, she announced, "I'm tired of this place. Come on, let's go!" she pulled him up.

"Are you taking me home?"

"No way! We're going to Yab. You'll like it there, I promise."

"Fine." He grabbed his jacket and followed her as she waved and said her good-byes to about half the people there. He hated to admit it, but he was already tired. He was bored, as much as he was tired. He did not like this woman, or the company that she kept. He could hear his mother telling him to stay away from women like that. "They are after your bed. And when she has her way with you, she'll throw you away like a Raggedy Andy doll." His mom taught him well, and at this moment he missed her more than ever. He promised himself he would call her in the morning.

The same ritual repeated itself when they arrived at the Yab lounge. There were no neon lights, but rather, a huge walnut door with the one word in caps, YAB, on the half-moon window. One half of the door was opened for her and her date allowing them to enter an even louder place but much smaller in size than the Full Up Club. The mirrors on the walls with the bright lights made it appear larger than it was. Once again, a bunch of people surrounded Evangelica and Dante. Once again, a Martini was placed on the table in front of her and Dante was asked what he wanted to drink. This time he asked for a Coke Zero.

"Do you want a shot of rum on the side?" some fake blonde asked.

"No thanks," Was his disappointing answer.

They stayed there for a little over an hour. Evangelica sulked the entire time. What a bore! I'm not getting anywhere with him. But she had something else in mind for later. Around one in the morning, she snapped her fingers again and gave the waitress her credit card. "Andiamo!" and once again she pulled Dante up to lead him out of there. Dante just did as he was instructed, wondering what her next move would be.

Once out on the street, she quickly made her way to the Hotel Bartolini, while tightly holding on to Dante. The modern glass doors parted as they entered.

"Wait, what are we doing here?" he stopped her.

"What do you think?" she tugged on his sleeve. "Isn't this what you've wanted all night long?" she gave him a suggestive look.

"Ummmm…no…what gave you that idea?" he thought she was rather presumptuous.

She turned to look him in the eyes. Her glare was flaming with anger that gave way to an alluring smile. "Don't you think I'm sexy? Don't you want to have sex with me?" he placed her hands on her hips.

"Listen Evangelica, you're one of the sexiest women I've ever met…"

"Okay, so what are we waiting for?" she pulled him closer to the elevators, but he wouldn't budge.

"…but no, I don't want to have sex with you." He pressed his lips together tightly and squinted, waiting for her to throw him a punch in the eye.

She winced, and then scowled at him. "Fine! Vafanculo!" she pushed him so hard he landed flat on his ass. She pranced out of there. The pounding her stilettos on the shiny marble floor echoed through the immense lobby.

Whew! That was close! There was no way he was going to compromise his job, his reputation, and most of all, his relationship with Serenella over some Italian spoiled brat. He pulled out his cell phone and called his uncle.

CHAPTER NINE

September 2020

As Dante said his good-byes to his aunt and uncle, he kept peeking over their shoulders to see if Serenella would come out of her apartment to wish him well. It wouldn't be good-bye, but rather farewell, because he would be coming back. He did not want to lose her. He had fallen in love with her and there was no way he was going to leave her in Italy. However, he had noticed that since that unfortunate incident with Evangelica, she had been very cold with him—even when he apologized profusely, trying to explain what happened. He had seen her only a few times out on the balcony and her attitude was distant and aloof.

"Dante, knock on her door. Do not be afraid. What's the worst that could happen?" Giuditta asked.

He inched towards her door and knocked lightly, while his aunt went inside followed by his uncle.

"Ciao," she said with a feeble smile as she appeared in the doorway.

"Ciao." He looked into her eyes, searching for a glimmer of hope. "I couldn't leave without saying ciao to you."

Serenella frowned. "I guess you mean addio."

"No, no, I mean arrivederci. I'm coming back."

She scoffed. "Why?"

He took her hands. "Because I love you, that's why. I want to be with you."

"Really? Well, what about that bitch, Evangelica? It was evident to me that you two hit it off quite nicely."

"No, we didn't...well...I didn't want to...she did...I just couldn't..."

She was disconcerted. "I saw you!"

"What?"

"I saw you leaving together! In her car! You seemed quite happy and excited to me."

"No, she was excited. She practically forced me to go out with her. I had no choice. Her father expected me to go out with her."

"Well, you know why, don't you?" she raised her eyebrows.

"Yes, of course I do. They want my company's leather..."

"And she wanted you as well."

"Well, I can promise you that she didn't get either."
He was becoming irritated, but he kept an even tone.

"No? Well, I thought…"

"You thought wrong." He pulled her hands to his lips. "I love you Serenella. I've loved you since the day I first laid eyes on you on the balcony. My feelings did not change just because I was forced to go on a date with that conniving snake. My mom raised me way better than that."

"I don't know if I can ever trust you again."

"Why do you say this?" he moved closer so to look straight into her chestnut eyes. "I have not been unfaithful to you, ever."

I want to believe him, I do but… "Addio Dante. I wish you all the best." She frowned a bit, did an about-face, and disappeared behind her apartment door.

"No…Serenella…no…" he stood there, slouching, for a good minute just staring at the number "2" on her door. For some odd reason, the number "2" was blurry. He rubbed his eyes, picked up his two suitcases, and started down the stairs.

Serenella, on the inside was also fighting back the tears. Her father's heart was breaking right along with his daughter's. He opened his arms. She flew into them, letting all her tears stream down. He hugged her tightly, not wanting to let his little girl go. It did not matter to him that she was not ten; he would always be there to protect her. He shook his head knowing that he could not prevent her heartbreak.

"I'm so sorry," was all that he could muster.

When Dante got out into the courtyard, he looked up at her balcony in the hopes of seeing the love of his life. But all he saw were the dangling pink and red geraniums.

"Come, Dante, we're going to be late." Alfredo had finished packing his trunk.

Saddened by her no-show, Dante slowly entered the small Italian car and buckled his seat belt.

Alfredo took off. "Come on Dante, there are plenty of fish in the sea."

No way! He took one last look at her apartment, watching the building become smaller and smaller, finally disappearing when Alfredo turned left to get on the main road leading to the highway. Perhaps I was a bit harsh, Alfredo thought as he drove. He hadn't realized Dante had fallen for his neighbor, but evidently, he was wrong. He turned on the radio and Adriano Celentano was playing. The piece was one of his favorites, "Venti-quattro Mila Baci" –Twenty-Four Thousand Kisses. He loved that tune.

At the airport, once he was through security, he texted Serenella.

Ciao! I miss you!

No answer.

Serenella, please forgive me. I love you.

Again, no answer.

Dante plopped his carry-on onto the floor, between his legs, and scooted it under the seat ahead. He tapped on his favorite playlist. Serenella had downloaded all her favorite songs on his music app and as he listened to each one raptly. Before and during the flight, and on his way home in the Uber, he couldn't hold back his tears, no matter how much he tried.

"Two weeks?" Sofia was flabbergasted as she dished out some more pasta for her only son.

"Yes, mom, I have to go to Brazil and then the Arab Emirates. After that, I'm going to India."

"India? Don't they have COVID over there?" Gianna asked.

"Yeah, I heard there's a large breakout in Brazil, too." AnnaBella commented.

"Come on girls, you're scaring your mom," Santo scolded them.

"Oh Signore! What kind of company sends their employees in countries where there are breakouts! This is insane. You need to quit, Dante! Right now!" Sofia was adamant.

Dante became infuriated. The moment he got out of the car, it was nag, nag, nag. He had been home only two hours, and he was ready to leave again.

"Basta!" Santo shouted. "Don't you see what you're doing? You are pushing him right out the door again. I can see it on his face." Santo got up and pulled his wife to sit next to him. "Now, sit here and calm down. Let him talk! Please, Sofia!"

"Fine, fine, I'll sit." And she made the gesture of locking her mouth with an imaginary key.

"Go on Dante."

"Guy is going to have me tested before I leave. If I test negative, I'll take the results with me. This seems to be the only requirement for Canadians."

"I'm so jealous! Brazil! That's definitely on my bucket list," Gianna exclaimed. "I'll bet you'll meet a lot of beautiful girls there, bro."

Dante's face darkened again.

"What's wrong Dante? You've been so glum ever since you got home." AnnaBella had noticed he was not himself.

"Nothin'." The chair made a scraping sound as he pushed away from the table. "I'm going to bed." He gently placed his napkin on his chair and pushed it in. "I'm really tired from the flight. Good night." He slumped over as he slowly made his way upstairs.

"What's wrong with him?" Sofia knew there was something going on. Dante was not acting right.

"Serenella."

"Serenella, who's she?"

"Zio Alfredo texted me while Dante was on the plane. Seems she is a young woman who lives next door and they fell in love."

"Ohhhh! Details Dad, details…" Gianna scooted up closer to her father.

Sofia scoffed. She got up and began gathering the dishes. She cleaned them, one by one, and loaded them into the dishwasher, huffing and puffing the whole time. She knew the whole story. Giuditta had kept her up to date. She was relieved that this relationship hadn't gone any further than it did. She was not ready for a daughter-in-law. Not yet anyway.

"Come on, mom! We want to hear the whole story!"

"Thank you, Gianna." Santo rolled his eyes at the behavior of his wife. "So, it seems they hung out a lot during the lockdown and they got really close. Then when some of the restrictions were lifted, they started dating."

"I see. So, why is he so glum?" AnnaBella asked.

"Well, from what I understand, he went out on a date with the daughter of a competing leather factory's owner, and Serenella saw them together."

AnnaBella slammed her fist on the table. "What an idiot brother I have!"

"Well, I'm glad they split up."

"Mom, why are you so cruel?"

"Well, be practical, Gianna. How will it work? Is she moving to Canada? Is he moving to Italy? Tell me. How is this love affair going to work?"

"Sofia, don't you remember when we were young?"

His wife suddenly became silent and hung her head in embarrassment.

"Why? What happened when you were young, dad?" AnnaBella asked.

"Well, I was supposed to go live in Texas and work with my best friend. Things were booming in Texas in the eighties and I would have made at least double what I made back then if I had moved to Texas."

"Wow!"

"But you didn't go, obviously."

"No, Gianna, I stayed in Ontario because I wanted to marry your mother." He got up to be with his wife. He kissed her on the cheek and put his arm around her shoulders. "See, Sofia, things have a way of working themselves out."

Sofia's heart melted. He was right. He had given up a lot for her. Not too many men would do that, not even back then. But Santo did. She looked at her husband. "I'm so glad you did that."

"It's because I love you, Sofia, and I still do." He kissed her passionately.

"Eww! Gross!"

They all laughed.

Dante heard the laughter coming from the kitchen. He wondered what was so amusing. He was so miserable. He turned on his phone. Eleven-twenty. It was really early over there. He texted her.

I know it's early there, but I really, really miss you. Do you miss me?

He waited a few seconds. No answer.

What can I do to earn your forgiveness?

Again, no answer.

He lay on his bed, closed his eyes, and thought back to the lockdown. In the midst of all the sadness of people getting infected and people dying, they were happy and healthy. He didn't sneeze or cough once during that whole time, and neither did she. All those good times came flooding back as he floated into a deep slumber.

~~~~~~

Serenella was in agony. He had been gone for three weeks, now, and she still could not get over him. Stupid! Stupid! She had scolded herself over and over again. You fell for him so quickly! Idiota! She picked up her phone and looked over Dante's text messages once again. Was he truly sorry? Could she trust him again? She looked at the pictures they took together. There were hundreds of them. Each one with Dante in it gently touched her, as if he were right there, next to her. But he wasn't, and he would never come back. She knew well he wanted to travel the world, not settle down with some plain Jane Italian girl. She had to let him go. He would be meeting hundreds of girls that looked just like Evangelica. She looked at herself in the mirror. "Oh, yes. I'm no match for her, not by a long shot."

"Serenella, dove sei?"

She went towards the voice she heard.

"Oh, ciao Giuditta." She said meekly.

"Tesoro!" she hugged the girl. "How are you holding up?"

At that question, she broke down and wept. Giuditta just held her and did not utter a word. She knew what the girl needed, and it wasn't her father. She needed a woman who understood exactly what she was going through. She held Serenella tightly and let her get her tears out while caressing her long dark hair.

"I miss him so much!" she exclaimed through the tears. "How did I fall for him like that?" she was sobbing, desperately trying to catch her breath.

Giuditta let her unload. She gently pulled her. "Come, I baked a Torta della Nonna and I have espresso ready to pour." They walked together out of her apartment and into Giuditta's apartment. "Now, sit and let's talk about Dante."

Serenella told Dante's aunt everything that was tucked away in her heart. She spoke for what seemed like a good hour without any interruptions. When she was done, Giuditta gave her a bit more of tough news.

"You know, as it is famously said, if you love someone, let them go. If he really loves you, he'll come back."

"How do I know that for sure?"

"You don't."

CHAPTER TEN

October 2020

Despite Sofia's objections, Dante left Canada for Brazil in early October. He felt bad for his mother, but he couldn't wait to be freed from her claws. Ever since he had come home, his mom was nonstop, twenty questions: where are you going? With whom? When are you coming home? Who is that friend of yours? And on and on. She was overbearing!

"Hey Guy, thanks for sending me to Brazil. I just couldn't stay home another minute."

"Hey man, don't mention it. I've been there."

"Cool. So, I'm boarding now. I'll let you know when I get there. Can you email me the contact info?"

"Sure thing."

The airport speaker squawked; first in English and then in French.

"Oh, gotta go." He hung up and placed his phone in his pocket while hurrying to get to his gate.

Brazil. The giant of Latin America. With its bountiful natural resources, including brazilwood, agriculture, and minerals, it has become the eighth largest economy in the world. He visited three different footwear factories, in Sao Paulo, Campinas, and Rio De Janeiro, negotiating great deals with the owners while they each wined and dined him. He discovered that Brazilian business culture is more informal than in Canada, putting a greater emphasis on personal relationships, which meant physical contact. He also discovered that being a handsome young Italian man made a great impression on the female business partners. He enjoyed Brazil enormously and loved the fact that they didn't require him to wear a mask.

A week later, he left Brazil and headed to India. The flight was exceptionally long, so he studied up on the Indian way of doing business. He read that when meeting an Indian person, the Namaste gesture, or the praying hand while bowing your head slightly, was quite common. He had to use his right hand for everything, as the left hand was considered unclean. Also, keeping your feet flat on the floor was important and pointing would be considered rude. He made sure he had plenty of business cards on hand. He visited seven different footwear and leather factories. These companies would settle for the second-grade leather as compared to the Brazilian companies, who wanted only top-of-the-line. The Indians wanted a better price; quality was not so important. This isn't as bad as it sounds, because LCD's second-grade is better than anyone else's top-grade. And he had plenty of all types and grades of leather samples with him to show off. The upper management of the Indian companies were the people making the decisions, and seniority is highly regarded. So, Dante made sure he spoke with the decision-makers at every company he visited. In most cases, Guy agreed to their terms.

Ten days later he flew to Vietnam, where an entire entourage of people was patiently awaiting his arrival. Right out of the airport, they took him to one of the fanciest hotels. They wined and dined him into oblivion. After only a few days of being in Hanoi, he was unable to stay focused between being sleep deprived and partied out. When he finally got on the plane, and was out of their sight, he passed out from the exhaustion.

South Korea was his next stop. He read up on their geopolitical stances. He discovered that Korea and Japan have a dispute of small islets called Dokdo or Takeshima as the Japanese would call them. If you wanted to impress the South Koreans, you did not speak of this issue so to not offend them in any way, as their response would be to abruptly end all business dealings. They are still a male-dominated business culture, while maintaining the upmost respect towards their female colleagues. He also learned not to be pushy with them, but rather to stay patient and gentle while being firm. Once he got there, the mask and social distancing mandate was in full force. He was not pleased with it but he had to go along. He discovered that they spoke English quite well. They were very polite to him, but he got the sense that they were nicely pushing the blade into his back while feeding him the best food and booze money could buy. He didn't realize it at first, but when he described what they were doing to Guy, he informed Dante of their kibun (their mood or inner feelings), and the best way of handle it: do not demand yes or no answers, but accept the need for slow, methodical decision-making. He warned him about contradicting someone openly or criticizing someone else, as a sure way to lose business. He advised Dante to give sincere compliments and to always show respect. In about a week he got the hang of it. and then it was time to leave.

He had never realized how high-quality his company's leather was, until he began to notice how much effort these business owners went through to get the best leather money could buy. Dealing with the diverse cultures and personalities, he became quite the negotiator and astute salesperson.

After hours of flying and looking out the aircraft window, the CN Tower suddenly came into view. A broad grin crawled across his face. When he saw the comparatively tiny Air Canada Centre, he wondered if he would ever see his Maple Leafs play, or his Toronto FC, or the Raptors, for that matter. He checked his phone and the only game that was scheduled was for the Toronto FC. But no spectators would be allowed. He shook his head. COVID had completely halted these favorite sports. Nonetheless, he was overjoyed to finally be home.

"Oh, Dante! I'm so happy you're home!"

Trying to wriggle his way out of her tight squeeze, he managed to say, "Me too, Ma. Me too." He let her hug him for a while. He figured she had suffered enough.

"So, tell us all about your travels." Sofia released him long enough so he could sit. Then she took the seat next to him and hugged him some more.

"Basta Sofia! You're suffocating him!" he forced her to let him go. "Now please, go make dinner."

"Dad! That's so chauvinistic of you!" AnnaBella glared at him.

Behind Sofia's back, Santo shrugged his shoulders while opening his hands, as if to day, "What!". Sofia got up to do as her husband had commanded, allowing AnnaBella to take her place.

"Yeah, Dante. Tell us about Brazil, bro." she handed her brother a Labatt's Blue that she had taken out of the fridge. "Cheers!" they clinked beer bottles along with Santo and Gianna.

Sofia was beaming. Her family was reunited again—and just in time. She wanted all three of her children to enjoy the traditions they had established over the years. Only one tradition would not be possible, and that was to go across the border into the U.S. for Black Friday shopping. If they did that, they would have to quarantine at home for fourteen days and that would interfere with the Fogli family Christmas house decorating, both inside and out, searching for the perfect tree, bringing it home, decorating it, and finally, having the entire family over for Christmas Eve and Christmas Day. Sofia already had the menu ready, not to mention that she had completed her Christmas shopping. She shopped all year long, just as she did before the pandemic. She had hidden the goodies at her mom's apartment at the Viaggio Finale nursing home. The only problem was how to retrieve those gifts now that the nursing homes were on lockdown again. She could only hope they would lift the restrictions by the time Christmas came, or she would be in deep trouble. Maybe she could sweet talk one of the nurses to bring her packages out to the lobby. She was exceptionally adept at that sort of thing.

They stayed up until nearly three in the morning, talking and eating and drinking beer. But when it was time to sleep, Dante was wide awake. He was still on South Korea time. His mind wandered to Serenella. He had been following her on Facebook and Instagram, but she didn't post much. Occasionally she'd post a photo of her with her father or her few friends that she had. She did go hiking up near L'Aquila where was showed off some fresh snow that had whitened the landscape. He did not see any men with her. That was good. He thought, I wonder what time it is over there? He picked up his phone. Four am meant ten in Florence. "What the hell…" he started a video call on WhatsApp.

"Dante? Why is he calling me?" she tightened her lips debating with herself whether or not to take the. She slowly hit the green answer button, biting her lower lip as Dante's face appeared.

"Serenella!" his smile stretched from ear to ear.

"Ciao Dante." She was overjoyed to see his face, but she could not give away her excitement.

He didn't think she would answer, and could hardly believe that she did. "You are so beautiful! I had almost forgotten how beautiful you are."

She cracked a smile as her cheeks turned the color of maraschino cherries. "So, how have you been?" she was barely able to muster.

"I'm good, now that I'm looking at you." Deep down he knew she missed him just the same as he did. He could see it in her eyes.

She stayed silent. Tears were welling in her eyes. She nodded and smiled.

"I've missed you so. I tried contacting you so many times, but when you didn't respond, I gave up. I'm sorry."

"Why are you sorry?"

"I shouldn't have. I should have insisted more. I'm sorry."

Serenella simply shrugged. She had a knot in her throat.

"I still love you, Serenella. I cannot stop thinking about you. I've been traveling all over the world for work and I've met so many people..."

"Lots of pretty girls, I'll bet."

"Yes, I'm not going to lie. There were a lot of pretty girls, but none can compare to you."

"You don't really mean that."

"Of course, I do. I've been honest with you the whole time. Never have I ever desired any woman other than you. Yes, I've seen a lot of pretty women during my travels but you..." he moved closer to the screen and gazed deeply into the camera so she could see his eyes. "...YOU are the only woman for me. I love you, Serenella. I love all of you. With all of me."

She decided Dante had suffered enough. Besides, she really didn't want this charade to continur, lest she lose him for good. She gave him a big smile. "Yes, I love you with all of me, too."

Dante pumped his fist in the air and yelled: "WOO-HOO! She loves me! She loves me!" he felt like that little Dante who had scored his favorite Star Wars action figure for Christmas. His mother really did a number on him when he was ten years old. She told him they couldn't afford such a pricy toy, but when he opened it on Christmas morning, he yelled out the same cry and gave everyone in his family a big warm hug. Especially his mother. Then he went outside, in his Star Wars pajamas to yell at the neighborhood what he had just received. He was ecstatic to say the least. And that was exactly how he felt now.

Serenella, too, was joyful. She missed Dante in nearly the same way she missed her mother after she passed away. She thought she had lost Dante forever, but now there was a glimmer of hope. "So, now what?" still smiling.

"What do you mean?" he was puzzled at that question.

"I mean, how do we continue? You are in Canada and I am in Italy. So, what now?"

Dante suddenly realized that their relationship was going to be challenging, to say the least. He wasn't sure how to answer her. "I honestly don't know. What about you? Any ideas?"

She tapped her index finger on her chin and stared at the screen. "Are you coming back to Florence for work?"

His eyes popped open at the thought of being in Italy again. "Wait, let me check." He pulled up his calendar but the frown on his face said everything. "No, sorry."

She had a thought. "Maybe, I could come to Canada?"

"Oh, that is an awesome idea." His smile stretched from ear to ear. He quickly went online to see if Italians could enter Canada. He sighed when he read that they couldn't, yet. "I'm so sorry, but we're not allowing Italians to come in just yet."

She was disappointed. She was already looking forward to seeing where he was born and raised. They talked a lot about Canada during those balcony meetings.

Dante was sad to see her disappointed face. "Don't worry Serenella. We will figure it out. I promise." He gave her a reassuring smile.

"I believe you."

"Good. What matters is that we're back together and I will not lose you. Never. I love you, Serenella, and we will be together, I promise." He was determined to keep that promise if it was the last thing he did.

"Okay, Dante, I must go now. Let's video chat tomorrow, okay?"

"Yes, of course." His screen went dark. He plugged his phone in and finally, he slept.

CHAPTER ELEVEN

November 2020

Dante was lounging around one day, aimlessly browsing the Internet. Suddenly, a phone call interrupted his reverie. He looked at the screen and saw Guy's face on the incoming call alert.

"Hi, Guy."

"Dante, I need you to go to northern Italy."

A broad grin crept across Dante's face. He felt as if he had opened the door to a bright, sunny day. "Really? When?" He didn't want Guy to catch on how he really felt so he kept his enthusiasm stifled.

"Well, you have to complete your two-week quarantine period, so when is that done?

"Three days, I think."

"Okay, good. Go ahead and book your flight to Milan. I'm going to send you all the details in an email shortly. Oh, and make sure you get tested immediately after your quarantine is over."

"Yessir, boss." I'll email you a copy of my itinerary."

Guy hung up and Dante jumped up and down for joy. He was going to see his precious girl again! He got online and searched for flights. He was amazed at how cheap they were. He began searching for hotels and then called Serenella.

She was feeling a bit down, but when she saw Dante's call come in, her mood changed. "Ciao Dante, come stai amore?"

"Ciao amore mio. How are you?"

"Much better now."

"Good. I have great news…"

"Really?"

"Yes. I'm coming to Milan next week." His excitement was bursting.

"You are? Milan?"

"Yes, but I'd like to meet you in Venice."

"Venice?"

"Yes. I've never been there, so I thought I could kill two birds with one stone."

"Oh, Venice is so romantic. Yes! Yes! Yes!" she couldn't contain her enthusiasm. She wanted to cheer, but there were customers in the store. She became serious again. "I must go now. We'll talk soon, yes?"

"Of course, my love."

He hung up and searched hotels in Venice. "Huh, this one looks interesting and the price is right. Sold!" he booked the hotel room. He was all set. Now, he just had to wait three more days. They were going to be long. Really long.

~~~~~~

"Is this the hotel?"

"Yes." He helped her out of the boat taxi. "Hotel La Serenissima. It has great reviews." He slung his bag over his shoulder, extended the handle of her small suitcase, and rolled it into the lobby.

"Wow! It's gorgeous!" She was excited to be in the most magnificent and charming city in Italy.

"Let's go in!" Dante was just as excited as she was— maybe more so.

The concierge greeted the couple. "Buongiorno signori. Posso essere d'aiuto?" Even though he was wearing a mask that bore the hotel's logo, the twinkle in his eyes and the way that they sort of scrunched up made it clear that he was smiling.

"Yes, Dante Fogli." He handed him his passport and pulled his mask down so that the gentleman could see his face.

"Oh, yes, Signor Fogli, we've been expecting you." Then he gave him a knowing look. "Will the young lady be joining you?"

"Yes."

"Very well, I would need her passport, please," assuming that Serenella was also from abroad.

Serenella pulled out her European passport and gave it to the Concierge.

"Molte grazie." He gestured her to lower her mask so he could see her face.

He hit some keys on his computer, closed both passports, and gave them back to their respective owners. Then he retrieved a fancy, old-fashioned key with a gondola shaped keychain attached, with "Hotel La Serenissima" engraved on it, and handed it to Dante. "Enjoy your stay."

"Grazie."

"Ragazzo, porta i bagagli per i signori alla stanza 205 per favore."

"Si, subito." A noticeably young, handsome bellboy quickly placed their few pieces of luggage onto a rack and headed for the elevator.

"Please follow the bellboy. He will take you to your room."

The couple simply nodded and followed the bellboy onto the elevator. Even with their masks on, they both knew well what each other was thinking. They held hands in anticipation of what was to come, once inside their room.

"Eccoci." The young man opened the door, set the key on the table, and rolled the cart in. He swiftly emptied it and rolled the cart out to the hallway.

"Here you go." Dante pressed a five Euro bill into the bellboy's hand as he left the room.

"Molte grazie Signore!" the bellboy disappeared as Dante closed the door and hooked the lock.

"Look at this view!"

Dante headed out onto the balcony. "Well, this is odd," he called out over his shoulder.

"Why do you say that?" She walked out to the balcony, wearing a quizzical look.

He turned around, wrapped his arms around her waist, and pulled her snugly against him. As he inhaled, he took in the subtle scent of her perfume. "We're actually on the same balcony for a change!"

Serenella laughed out loud and lifted herself onto her tiptoes to kiss him on the lips. "This is crazy—you know?"

"Yes, I know." With his arms still wrapped around her, he gently maneuvered her into the room, shutting the balcony doors behind them. Standing right in front of her, he pulled her even more tightly, as if that could be possible, and kissed her passionately. "Finally, you will be mine, my love. I want you so much. I want to get to know every part of you—inside and out." He removed his heavy sweater, throwing it across the room with abandon. "Will you let me?" he peeled his white cotton t-shirt over his head and flung it so that it landed almost next to the sweater.

"Yes, Dante. I'm all yours." She followed Dante's gestures, unbuttoning her coat to reveal a soft cotton t-shirt.

His hand glided under the t-shirt, causing her body to quiver—tightening and then relaxing, as he cupped her perfectly-shaped breasts in his hands. Like tiny secrets, he felt the hard pearls of her nipples against the palms of his hands.

Her heart seemed to stop. Her breath came in gasps. Now, all she could muster were moans of pleasure.

He pulled her toward the bed, slowly undressing her. He could feel her breaths coming heavily, and he noticed a tinge of red blossoming on her cheeks. He began to negotiate the button on the waistband of her jeans, and then the zipper. Finally, free, he slipped his fingers underneath the elastic of her panties and slowly slid them down while ever-so-gently sliding both hands down the sides of her legs. She inhaled suddenly, but briefly.

"Serenella, I've been waiting so long. I can't wait any longer."

"Then don't. Her voice cracked, coming out between gasps"

Fully and completely, Serenella surrendered to him. She pulled him onto herself. As they kissed, a fire ignited between them. A fire that there was only one way to extinguish!

He wrapped one strong hand around the back of her head, her silky hair intertwined with his fingers, and thrust himself deeply into her.

"Oh!" she said between her moans. She wanted all of him, immediately, and she was not prepared to wait. She pushed herself fiercely against him, allowing him to take her fully and completely. She began to grind her hips up and down, filling herself with him, holding him at the back of his neck for leverage.

Dante lifted her leg just enough so she could feel his strength. Her whole body became weaker as she felt a familiar wave of pleasure roiling up within her. She met his thrusts with her own as she edged closer and closer. The waves of pleasure began to mount for both as they progressed into convulsions that gripped Dante as he held his rhythm, bringing him closer to his peak.

They held each other more tightly, Serenella's fingernails dug into Dante's neck; he pulled her hair, tilting her head to the side, which allowed him to nibble and kiss her neck. They were staring at each other, stoking that ardent fire while their moans became louder and louder.

Finally, Serenella allowed the wave to crash down on her. Every muscle seized, hot convulsions shattering her whole body! She breathed obscenities through her teeth which heightened Dante's passions. He finally lost himself, releasing a visceral groan as he climaxed inside her orgasm-wracked body.

Exhausted, they slumped into each other, smiling and catching their collective breath.

"Mamma mia!" he exclaimed while still breathing heavily.

"Yes, indeed."

She laid her head on his chest and dozed off soundly, and most of all, happy.

~~~~~~

Serenella felt her stomach growl, so she gently awakened Dante. "Hey, signore…"

He groaned and stretched a bit. "Mmmmm."

"Are you hungry?"

He had to think about that for a moment, but then, right on cue, his stomach growled. "Um, yes, now that you mentioned it.…"

About ten minutes later, they were walking hand-in-hand across St. Mark's Square.

"What about that place?" Dante asked.

"Café Busetto? Sure, why not?"

As they sat down, a quite handsome, dark-haired man approached them. "Buon pomeriggio." He gave her a not-so-subtle, flirty smile. "What can I get you today?"

Dante did not like the looks of this scoundrel. "Menu please," he said in a guarded tone.

When the waiter heard him speak in English, he smiled from ear to ear. "Ah, American?"

"No, Canadian."

"Your English is very good." Serenella figured he had learned by dealing with Americans all his life, since he appeared to be Venetian.

"Well, you can thank my wife for that. She's American, you know."

A little more relaxed, Dante stated, "American? Well, I'll bet she's beautiful."

"No, my friend, she's absolutely gorgeous!" He turned to look at the window of the glass shop and pointed. "And she's right over there."

As if on cue, the young couple both turned toward the shop. They saw a beautiful blonde waving back at the waiter, smiling and rubbing her extended tummy.

"She is beautiful."

"Yessir, you're a lucky man."

"I am." He turned. "I'll be back with the menus in a moment."

Just before he walked into his shop, he blew a kiss to his wife. A few moments later, he brought out two menus.

"Her glass pieces look very interesting."

"Oh, yes, my Tiffany is extremely talented. You should go visit after you are done here and tell her that Massimo sent you. She will give you a discount. I promise."

"Oh, I might take you up on that." Serenella suddenly became excited about the prospect of finding an extraordinary piece that would remind her of her visit to Venice.

As soon as Dante paid the tab after their meal, he took Serenella's hand and they headed toward the glass shop.

"Buongiorno." A very obviously pregnant Tiffany greeted them.

"Salve, come va?" Serenella replied.

"I understand you're American." Dante spoke in English.

"Yes," she smiled. "You were talking to my very handsome husband, weren't you?"

"Yes, we were. He said you'd give us a discount."

"Of course. It's a pleasure to find fellow Americans."

"Oh, I'm Canadian."

"Oh, are you now! Where from exactly?"

"Woodbridge, Ontario. Very close to Toronto."

"Oh, I'll bet it's very lovely this time of year."

"It is."

"Oh, I miss home. I'm from just outside of Seattle. The colors are spectacular this time of year. Too bad I can't go." She rubbed her tummy. "I really wanted this baby to be born in the States, but oh well, I guess I'll have to wait for his brother or sister." She sounded frustrated, but she kept her spirits high. "So, please look around and let me know if you see anything you like."

"Dante, look at this one." Serenella had already found a gondola with an unbelievable array of colors, that appeared to be floating on the canal.

"It is beautiful and very original. I've always seen those plastic toy gondolas. But never something like this."

"Ha ha ha! Yes, the toy ones are made in China now. Everything is made in China, but not these. These are all hand made by me, right here in this shop." Tiffany went to pick it up. "Let's see what I can do for you."

"The price says two hundred Euros." Serenella couldn't possibly spend that kind of money.

"Okay, how about one hundred and fifty?"

"We'll take it!" Dante already had his card out.

"But…"

"No, amore. you like it. It's yours." He handed the card to Tiffany.

Tiffany cashed him out and gave the bag with the Gondola to Serenella. "Thank you so much and enjoy Venezia!"

Dante put his arm around his lover and winked at Tiffany. "Oh, we will."

CHAPTER TWELVE

December 2020

Finally, the Fogli family was able to get on that flight to Italy. It would be an overnight flight that would arrive at eight the next morning. Sofia couldn't be happier. She was about to hug her son. Thirty days! Thirty long days she had waited to be able to again embrace her firstborn. It seemed to her that 2020 had mostly been made up of long periods of waiting. She was excited, but she was also impatient, and these two opposing feelings were turning her into a "travelzilla."

"Mom, you've got to calm down," Gianna commented. "You're not getting there any faster if you act like this. Just relax. You'll see him soon enough."

Santo waited patiently for their luggage to arrive. He couldn't understand why his three girls needed so much luggage. All he brought was a Juventus duffle bag and his toiletry bag. But the women…oh no…they needed two suitcases. Each. Why? As the luggage reached him, he pulled them off the carousel and onto the floor, counting as he set them in line. One…two…three… and finally, six. "Okay, let's go!" he barked, as they cackled among themselves.

As the entourage exited Amerigo Vespucci Airport, they tore off their masks and made their way to the pick-up curb so they could hurry up and wait some more. All sorts of people were coming and going, all masked up, and all impatiently waiting to get to their destinations. Santo was surprised to see so many people in December. *I guess people are tired of staying home. They've had enough, just like me.*

"There he is!"

"Dante!"

"Hi mom!" He gave her a warm hug, holding on for what seemed like a week! Then he moved over to the left a bit, revealing Serenella standing behind him. "Mom, Dad, AnnaBella and Gianna, this is Serenella."

Santo noticed his wife turn white as a sheet of paper. He immediately took her hand and squeezed it. Dante's sisters both rushed to hug Serenella.

"So, happy to meet you."

"Yes, we've heard so much about you." Gianna then whispered in her ear. "Welcome to the family."

"Come on mom, let me help you into the van."

"This little thing is a van?" Santo was almost scandalized at that little square vehicle. "This looks like a toaster!"

"Yes, dad, things aren't so big here in Italy, you know," he grinned.

Sofia did not say a word. She just made herself as comfortable as she could in the back seat. She looked straight ahead with a blank expression on her face.

"You think she's in shock?" Gianna whispered to AnnaBella, to which she simply nodded. "Oh boy."

Santo finally broke the awkward silence. "So, Serenella, tell us about yourself."

"Yes, we want to know every detail!" AnnaBella added.

"Of course." Serenella spoke in English. She was relieved that she was well accepted, except for Dante's mother. Dante had warned Serenella about her. Sofia was eerily quiet, making Serenella uncomfortable. "Ask me whatever you want."

The twenty questions began and there were many more, too, especially from the two girls. They wanted to know every detail about their brother's girlfriend. They both loved the answers they got, and they were both extraordinarily excited to have this modern Italian woman in their brother's life. The elephant in the room needed to be addressed, though, but that could wait—for now.

Giuditta had lunch ready for the Canadians. She prepared La Pappa Con Pomodoro, Florentine Fried Chicken, and mixed steamed vegetables. For dessert, she baked Torta Della Nonna.

"Oh Giuditta, I had forgotten how good your cooking is!"

"Thank you, Santo."

Everybody in the room agreed with Santo except Sofia. Giuditta had a good idea why her sister-in-law was quiet. She whispered something in Alberto's ear and took off her apron.

"Vieni Sofia, andiamo a fare una passeggiata."

"No, I'm too tired to walk."

"No, no, you're coming. We need to catch up." She gave Sofia her heavy sweater. "Dai su."

Reluctantly Sofia got up, took the sweater that was offered to her and went with Giuditta. Once they were in the courtyard, Giuditta confronted her sister-in-law.

"Now, please tell me what's wrong. You haven't said a word since you got here."

"Oh, nothing," she pouted.

"Nothing? Is that nothing's name Serenella?"

Sofia shrugged.

"I thought so. Sofia, you have got to let Dante go. He's thirty, now. He is a man. He has to make his own path in life."

"I know. But bringing HER to meet us at the airport? That was uncalled for."

"Why? You knew about her. I told you many times that they were seeing each other."

"Yes. But bringing her to the airport. That was wrong. I just wanted to see Dante, not HER."

Giuditta hooked her arm into Sofia's. "Listen, cogna, I hear you, I do. When Riccardo moved up north, I was devastated. And not even a few months passed, and boom! A girlfriend, too."

"Oh, I didn't know."

"Of course, you didn't. I didn't express my feelings to anyone. I had to accept it. He left at twenty-two, but he was offered a good job. He really could not turn it down, especially since good jobs in Italy are very hard to find. I had to let him go."

"I see."

"Then he met Raffaella, and the next Christmas he brought her home. Once again, I had a choice to make; it was either accept her or risk losing my son. In the end, she is not so bad. It could have been much worse. But she works in a bank and he is a foreman at the Ferrero factory. I could not have asked for more for my son. At least you have your girls. I have only Riccardo."

As they walked along the busy Florentine street, the two women huddled together so they could warm up. Sofia breathed in the crisp air.

"Feeling better?"

She nodded.

"Let me tell you something, Sofia. I wish my Riccardo were dating Serenella. She is such a wonderful young woman. She took care of her father when her mother passed away from cancer. All she did until she met Dante was work and come home to take care of Bruno, her father. She is strong and fierce. I promise you; you'll grow to love her. Give her a chance."

"Well…" she cracked a smile. "she really is a beautiful girl."

"There you go. Remember, you're not losing a son; you're gaining a daughter."

"And I'll bet they will make beautiful grandbabies."

"Ah, yes, and you're going to make a wonderful grandmother."

"Nonna. That has a nice ring to it."

~~~~~~

The next day, when Serenella left for work, Dante knocked on Bruno's door.

When Bruno saw it was Dante, his expression turned dour. "What do you want?"

"Signor Bruno, may I come in? I need to speak with you."

Bruno gestured him to enter. "Anything to drink?"

"No, thank you."

Bruno noticed he was fidgeting with his hands, his jacket zipper, and putting his hands in his pockets and then taking them out. "Out with it. What's going on?"

"I...um...I..."

Bruno placed his hands on his hips and stuck out his chest which made him look even more imposing.

"I came today to-to a-ask for Serenella's hand in marriage."

Bruno's ego deflated as he sat down. "Marriage?"

"Yes." Dante sat, also.

"Did you ask her yet?"

"No, I want to do this the right way. I want your blessing first."

"If I may ask, are you taking her away from me?"

"Oh no, I'll be moving to Florence. I would never take her away from you. If she accepts my proposal, I'd like to find an apartment close by."

Bruno had mixed feelings. He was ecstatic that his daughter was getting married, but saddened that she would not be living with him. She had been his pillar, ever since his wife died, and now comes this American to take her away. But hopefully, he is going only a few blocks away. He did like Dante. He noticed how Serenella had changed since the day they met, and she has been very docile ever since. "All right, you may."

"I may?"

"Yes, you may marry my daughter." He smiled at this young man who was more traditional than most young Italian men he knew. He got up and extended his hand.

Dante shot up and hugged his future father-in-law. "Thank you, Bruno, thank you! I promise I'll take good care of your daughter."

Bruno felt his warmth. He knew deep in his heart that Dante was going to make a good husband for his precious Serenella. "You had better."

~~~~~~

Dante took Sofia into the historic part of Florence. He wanted to dedicate some time to his mom to try and convince her of his intentions for his beloved. They visited the Palazzo degli Uffizi Gallery and the Accademia Gallery where the immense and powerful statue of David is located.

"My God! Michelangelo was a true genius!" Sofia was taking dozens of photos of the masterpiece. "You know, Dante, the cameras on these phones nowadays are spectacular! There's no need to spend hundreds of dollars on a camera."

Dante already had his chance to marvel at the statue with Serenella, but he still enjoyed his mother's reaction. It was priceless. He grabbed his mother's phone and snapped a few photos of her next to some of the masterpieces, to add to her memories of this trip.

Later in the afternoon, they browsed the jewelry shops on Ponte Vecchio. This was what Dante really had come for; to search for a ring to present to his lovely Serenella. Before they walked on the bridge, Sofia bought gelato for them both. It was rather cool, but Italian gelato good all year 'round, no doubt.

"Wow, this gelato is amazing! Oh, and look at these shops! They are spectacular!"

As Dante licked his cone, slurping and smacking his lips as he savored the gelato, he wandered over to one of the jewelry shops. "Mom, did you know that these shops are more than five hundred years old?"

"No, I didn't." She followed her son.

"Look at that one. What do you think?" he pointed to a white gold, diamond clustered engagement ring.

Sofia peered at him and gave him a clever look. She knew. "For Serenella, I assume?"

"Yes, yes. But what do you think of that one?" He moved his finger to another ring that sat just above the first one. This one was pink gold that had brown and white diamonds, with the major diamond in the center standing out from the rest.

"Oh, I like that one better."

"Should I go in and ask how much it is?"

"Of course, but I think you should finish your gelato first. You know these jewelers may be a bit snooty when it comes to food and jewelry."

"Yeah, I guess you're right." He headed for a marble bench that was located towards the middle of the bridge.

Sofia sat next to her son. "So, you want to propose?"

Dante looked at his mother's face expecting to find it annoyed. Except he didn't. She was smiling warmly. "Yes."

"Okay," was all she said as she finished polishing off her gelato al ciocolato.

"Really? That's it? Okay? No objections?" he was puzzled to say the least.

Sofia got up to throw away her stained napkins, then took her place next to her son again. "Yes, Dante. That's it. You're a man now and I don't have any say as to who your wife should be."

He cocked his head.

"Who are you and what have you done with my mother?"

They both laughed wholeheartedly. "Good. Now that we've cleared this up, let's go buy an engagement ring, shall we?"

"I'm going to buy it Mom. Not we. Okay?"

"Absolutely, but if it's a bit above your pay grade, I'll put in the rest. Deal?"

"Deal." He kissed his mom and gave her a warm hug.

Tears streamed down her face as Dante opened the door for his mother.

"Buongiorno, signori. Posso essere d'aiuto?" The elderly salesman asked.

"Si, vorremmo vedere quel anello li in vetrina." Dante pointed to the window.

"Si, certo, quale?"

Dante pointed at the second ring, smiling from ear to ear.

~~~~~~

"All right everyone. Before we begin, please join me in prayer." Giuditta held out her hands to be joined by her husband and son. The entire entourage joined hands and bowed their heads.

"God of all gifts, we thank you for the many ways you have blessed us this day. We are grateful for each person gathered around this table. We ask you to bless us and our food, and to bless those we love who are not with us today. In our gratitude and love we remember your humble birth into our lives and pray for those who cannot enjoy Christmas with their families due to the pandemic. We bless you and give you thanks in your Spirit who brings our hearts to life this Christmas day and forever. Amen."

A loud "Amen!" echoed around the table.

"Buon Natale, e buon appettito!" Giuditta shouted as she placed the traditional Christmas dishes, she had prepared on the extended dining room table. It was adorned with red and white tablecloth, napkins. A Christmas centerpiece made of pine branches, red and gold ribbon, and gold candles added the finishing touch.

The spread consisted of Tuscan sausage, pasta, Tuscan-style roasted leg of lamb, and roasted potatoes—along with steamed vegetables, a diverse variety of cheese, and for dessert—pandoro and panettone.

"You have outdone yourself, my talented wife!" Alfredo exclaimed while he picked up the huge pasta dish and passed it around.

"Mmmmm smells delicious!" Riccardo closed his eyes to take in the aroma of his mother's pasta.

Even though the room was small, many people were gathered, and Giuditta was ecstatic beyond all measure. The chatter, the clinking of cutlery, the ooh-ing and ahh-ing of her culinary skills filled her heart with joy. Her son brought Raffaella to officially meet his parents. As it turned out, she fit right in with the rest of the family. Dante and his family were present. Bruno and Serenella were also invited. Giuditta couldn't wait to see how the young lady would react. Even Dante's boss, Guy Marchetti, was there. He was going through an exceptionally rough divorce and needed the warmth of family to get him through the holidays. Giuditta really liked Guy and wondered how any woman would want to divorce him. In that moment, it really didn't matter; what mattered was that everyone was enjoying themselves and that they were celebrating the coming of the baby Jesus, which meant much needed hope after such a difficult year.

Alfredo rose from his seat at just about dessert time. "Everyone, please, if I may say a word."

A hush descended over the group.

"Grazie!" he cleared his throat and raised his spumante flute. "I'd like to personally thank you for coming into my humble home. I have never had so many people here, and I am profoundly grateful that you all are here, especially with the difficulties of this past year. But let us not dwell on the past. Let us look cheerfully toward the future, and although uncertain, we can still cherish the bad along with the good. After all, it is the bad times that make us enjoy the good times even more. Here's to family and friends! Auguri! Buon Natale a tutti! Merry Christmas to all!"

Everyone clapped joyfully and clinked their spumante flutes. As the Pandoro platter was passed around, Dante rose and reached his hand for Serenella's.

This is it! Sofia thought.

A few other people in the room knew exactly what was about to happen.

"In a way, I am grateful for this pandemic. It brought me here and, by locking us down I was able to meet and fall in love with Serenella. I was angry at first, but then our long talks about all sorts of things mellowed me out and gave me a different perspective. The time away from you was excruciating, but when I saw you on my phone late that night, I knew that I was not going to be away from you, ever again. Simply put, I love you, Serenella and I want to spend the rest of my life with you."

When Dante knelt on one knee and pulled out a small blue velvet box, tears flowed down her cheeks, like tiny Tuscan creeks. She never imagined this. Never in a million years!

"Serenella Torretti, mi fai l'onore di diventare mia moglie?" he asked as he opened the little blue velvet box to reveal a white and brown diamond cluster ring that shone as brightly as his love for her.

With a lump in her throat, she mustered a faint "Yes."

"Yes?"

"Yes, Dante, I'll marry you." She rubbed the tears away, but more followed.

Everyone cheered with delight and each person stood to congratulate the couple. Finally, when the couple was able, they kissed to seal their new commitment to each other.

"Dante how are we going to do this?" she pulled him into the bedroom hallway.

"What do you mean?"

"I mean, where are we going to live? Here or in Canada?"

"Well, would you be interested in moving to Canada?"

She thought about that for a minute. "I really don't know. I'd like to see Canada, but I cannot leave my father."

"Then, it's settled. We will live here, and then maybe later, we can move to Canada. We will play it by ear. What do you say?"

"I say yes." She kissed him on the cheek. "You know, we don't have to worry about where to live, we can live with Papà for a while."

He really wasn't thrilled about that, but he didn't want to upset his fiancée, so he nodded in agreement. "Okay, now that we've settled that, let's go have some espresso."

"Good idea."

When they went back to the table and sat down, the congratulations were repeated all over again, and more spumante was passed around in celebration.

"So, have you decided on a date yet?" Gianna asked.

"And will you be moving to Canada?" Sofia asked Serenella with a glimmer of hope in her eye.

"Mom, we're staying here, in Florence because Serenella doesn't want to leave her father alone." Then he turned to Bruno. "Will that be all right with you?"

Bruno beamed with happiness. "Of course, it is all right. I will be happy to babysit my grandchildren when you two are working." He gave his daughter a knowing wink.

"Papà, there will be time for that."

"I know, I know…whenever you are ready."

Serenella rolled her eyes.

"So, the date, Dante. When is the date?"

"Oh, Gianna, I don't know, maybe next spring?" He turned to his fiancée. "What do you think about that? Too soon?"

"Oh, spring is fine." She smiled warmly as he embraced her.

"Well, you know what they say," Santo proclaimed.

"What?" everyone answered at the same time.

"Good things always happen in springtime," he said proudly.

Everyone burst out laughing.

"All right, now that we've settled that, how about a game of Tombola?"

"Yes! I want card numbers four and six. They are my lucky numbers," Sofia said, excitedly.

"My goodness! You still use those cards?"

"Yep, and get ready, 'cause I'm going to win, win, win!"

THE END

I truly hope you enjoyed this novella...

As an indie...

...(independent) author, I rely on reviews. In fact, those gold stars are the indie authors' lifelines. If you truly care about your favorite indie author, or any other indie, please leave a review on at least one of the following websites:

Amazon - www.Amazon.com

Barnes & Noble - www.barnesandNoble.com

BookBub- www.Bookbub.com

Goodreads - www.Goodreads.com

Google Books - https://play.google.com

iBooks App - https://iBooks.com

Thank you so much for your support. Do not forget, I write for you!

Merry Christmas from your favorite author,

Joanne Fisher

And now, an excerpt from Joanne Fisher's

second murder mystery

The Melbourne Connection

Something wasn't sitting right with Sid. He really did not want to get involved, because Nora was his son's girlfriend. But on the other hand, he felt obligated. The girl's mother had been killed and a body was never found. It could be anywhere from Melbourne, Australia to Melbourne, Florida. Finding her killer was going to be a huge undertaking. He would have to travel to Australia—and heck, that was a sixteen-hour flight! With his bladder? That flight was going to be a killer! But a woman's life was taken, and he had become quite fond of that woman's daughter. I'll do it, he thought. And now he had to let his son and Nora know his intentions, but he had no clue how to begin the conversation. He wondered if Janice was willing to sweeten the deal with one of her wonderful Italian meals. It was worth a try. He pulled out his cell, found his wife's number: 01 Wife Janice, and hit Call.

"Hey, Sid."

"Hey honey. Listen, I have to ask you something."

"Hummm, let me guess...you want to find Nora's mother's killer."

"But how?"

"Oh, come on, Sid! How long have we been married?"

"I know, but how did you figure it out?"

"Honey, Nora is dating Junior and I know that you've taking a liking to her. Haven't you?"

"Yes."

"Well, I saw the other night, when she started talking about how her mother died, and how her body was never found, and how she never understood why she was killed, that spark in your eyes reappear."

Sid's heart filled with even more love for his wife of 37 years. She knew him inside and out, right side up and upside down, and she was always one step ahead of him. He never figured out how she did it. "Do you know how amazing you are?"

Janice smiled. "Yeah, yeah, I know," verbally waving him off.

"I'm on my way home. Do I need to pick anything up?"

"Nope. I'll dig up your passport."

"What for?" "Well, duh! You'll be traveling to Australia, right?"

OTHER BOOKS

By Joanne Fisher

1.   With All of Me

2.   With All of Me II

3.   Her Spanish Doll

4.   Good Things Always Happen in Springtime

5.   Baker's Dozen Anthology

6.   The Devil of St. Gabriel

7.   Magnolia Blossom

8.   Christmas in Venice

9.   Traveling Boomers – First Stop Italy

10. Traveling Boomers – Second Stop Israel

ABOUT THE AUTHOR

Joanne Fisher is a Canadian-Italian-American author who is renowned for her steamy romances, her historical fictions and her murder-mysteries. She has also penned two non-fiction travel guides titled Traveling Boomers, along with the corresponding website www.TheTravelingBoomers.com. She has also participated in several Space Coast Writers Guild anthologies and has written one of her own, Baker's Dozen Anthology, which is free on Kindle Unlimited. She is the President of the Space Coast Writers' Guild and lives in Central Florida with her hubby, Dan and two Dachshunds, Wally and Madison.

And now, some authentic Florentine recipes

Penne Strascicate

Ingredients:

3 stalks celery

2 medium carrots

1 red onion

2 ounces pancetta

1/2 cup extra-virgin olive oil

1/2 pound ground beef

1/2 pound ground pork

1/2 pound ground veal

1 cup pinot grigio or another Italian white wine

3 pounds canned San Marzano peeled tomatoes

Salt and pepper

4 ounces (1 stick) salted butter, cut into pieces

1 1/2 pounds penne pasta

6 ounces freshly grated Parmigiano Reggiano

Instructions:

Finely chop the celery, carrots, onion and pancetta. Sauté the chopped mixture in the olive oil in a large skillet over medium heat until golden. Add the ground beef, pork and veal and continue to sauté until the meat is cooked. Add the white wine and cook until evaporated.

Puree the tomatoes in a blender and add them to the meat mixture. Season the meat mixture with salt and pepper and continue to cook over a medium heat until the sauce has thickened, at least 1 1/2 hours.

Bring 4 to 6 quarts water to a boil in a large pot. Add 3 teaspoons salt. Add the pasta and cook, stirring occasionally, until al dente, 10 to 11 minutes. Drain the pasta and add it to the sauce. Add the butter and cook until melted and the pasta is coated, 1 to 2 minutes. Garnish the pasta with the Parmigiano Reggiano before serving.

Arista All Fiorentina

https://www.bigoven.com/recipe/arista-alla-fiorentina/456400

Ingredients:

3 Lbs. Pork Loin Roast

6 Cloves Garlic, run through press

1 tsp Thyme, fresh

1 tsp Italian seasoning

1 tsp salt

1 teaspoon ground black pepper

2 to 3 tablespoons extra virgin olive oil

3/4 cup Marsala wine

1/4 cup Dry Vermouth

1 Envelope Knorr brown gravy mix

1/2 cup Water

Instructions:

In a small bowl, combine thyme, Italian seasoning, pepper, salt, garlic, and enough oil to form a paste. Spread on all sides of roast. Wrap roast in plastic wrap and let it marinate overnight. Preheat oven to 450°F. Place roast, fat side up, in a roasting pan or oven safe dish. Roast for 25 minutes, then reduce heat to 350°F and continue to roast approximately 30-60 minutes more until a thermometer placed in center reads 140°F. Remove roast from pan and tent with aluminum foil. Meanwhile, place roasting pan over stove burner and deglaze pan using Marsala and Vermouth, using whisk to scrape up all brown bits. On another burner, place small saucepan over medium heat. Add water and brown gravy mix. Pour Marsala vermouth mixture through a fine mesh sieve into gravy mix and continue to cook until it comes to full boil, then cook at low a few minutes more. Meanwhile, carve roast to desired thickness and serve with sauce. Serves approximately 6 people.

Pappa Al Pomodoro

https://www.196flavors.com/italy-pappa-al-pomodoro/

Ingredients:

2 Lbs. tomatoes (or high quality canned peeled tomatoes)

¾ lb. stale Tuscan bread, sliced

4 cups vegetable broth

1 bunch basil

2 cloves garlic

1 tsp sugar

Salt to taste

Fresh ground black pepper

2 TBSP Extra virgin olive oil

Instructions:

If using fresh tomatoes

Bring water to a boil in a large pot.

Turn tomatoes over and cut two small shallow incisions cross shape.

Boil tomatoes for 4 minutes.

Remove, let cool then peel.

If using fresh bread

Place slices on baking sheet lined with parchment paper.

Bake at 300 F / 150 C for 10 minutes, turning over the slices after 5 minutes.

Let cool.

Rub slices with garlic.

Place the slices of bread in a large pan.

Pour in the tomatoes and the vegetable stock so that the slices of bread are totally covered.

Add the sugar and cook over low heat for 40 to 50 minutes, until the liquid is fully evaporated.

Stir occasionally to allow even cooking and to help the bread break down and absorb the liquid.

Season with salt and pepper.

Remove from the heat.

Serve in individual bowls and pour olive oil to taste. Garnish with basil leaves.

Bistecca alla Fiorentina (Tuscan Porterhouse)

https://www.allrecipes.com/recipe/135541/bistecca-alla-fiorentina-tuscan-porterhouse/

Ingredients:

1 beef porterhouse steak (2.5 lbs.) Separable lean and fat trimmed

4 sprigs rosemary, fresh

3 TBSP Extra Virgin Olive Oil

1 pinch Sea Salt

6 lemon wedges, raw with peel

Instructions:

Press chopped rosemary onto both sides of porterhouse steak; set onto a plate and allow to marinate at room temperature for one hour.

Start an outdoor grill using hardwood charcoal, such as hickory. When coals are white and glowing, arrange for high heat.

161

Gently brush or rub olive oil onto steak, then season to taste with sea salt and pepper.

Place steak onto grill and cook until a dark, golden brown (not burnt) crust forms, five to 10 minutes depending on thickness of meat. Turn over, and continue cooking until golden on the other side, five to ten minutes more. When finished, place steak onto a platter and allow to rest for ten minutes.

To serve, remove the two pieces of meat from the bone, and replace the bone onto the serving platter. Trim any unwanted fat from the round (tenderloin) steak, slice into 6 equal pieces at an angle to the grain, and fan out on one side of the bone. Slice the rectangular (loin) steak into 1/4-inch slices at an angle to the grain. Fan out on the other side of the bone. Finish by garnishing the platter with lemon wedges and a sprinkle of additional sea salt.

Torta Della Nonna

https://wordpress-344121-1308337.cloudwaysapps.com/torta-della-nonna/

Ingredients:

Pastry

250 grams cake flour or 00 flour

1 egg large

3 yolks

100 grams sugar

3 tablespoons butter

3 tablespoons extra-virgin olive oil melted with the butter

1/2 teaspoon pure vanilla extract

Filling

250 grams ricotta fresh

125 grams pine nuts

125 grams sugar

1 lemon zest and juice

3 eggs

Instructions:

Preheat the oven to 400 F.

Make a well in the flour and put the egg, yolks, sugar, butter and olive oil mix into the center to make a stiff dough, similar to fresh pasta.

Take your time and don't stress.

Add the flour little at a time until the liquid in the well is thick enough to bring together with your hands.

Knead until the dough is smooth and allow it to rest for about 20 minutes in the fridge.

Make the filling by mixing together the ricotta, pine nuts, sugar, lemon zest, lemon juice and eggs in a bowl until you have a creamy mixture.

Roll out the pastry into two circles.

Put one circle down to line the bottom and sides of your pan.

Spread the ricotta mixture evenly over this layer and then put the other circle of dough over the top and nip the edges together.

Put in the oven to bake for 35 to 40 minutes, keeping an eye on it.

Remove and serve warm or at room temperature.

Serve with a Vin Santo from Cappezzana.

Note: Prep time fifteen minutes. Cook time forty minutes. Rest time twenty minutes. Serving slices: ten.

Biscotti di Prato (Cantucci)

https://www.foodandwine.com/recipes/cantucci-di-prato

Ingredients:

3 cups all-purpose flour

1 cup granulated sugar

1 cup sliced almonds

2 tsp baking powder

2 tsp anise seeds

Finely grated zest of lemon

¼ tsp salt

3 large eggs

2 egg yolks

2 tsp holy wine (vin santo or other sweet wine)

1 large egg white (lightly beaten)

Instructions:

Preheat oven to 350°F. Line a baking sheet with parchment paper. In a mixing bowl with a paddle, combine flour with one cup of sugar, almonds, baking powder, anise seeds, lemon zest and salt. Add the whole eggs, egg yolks and holy wine. Beat at low speed until a stiff, crumbly, slightly sticky dough forms.

Turn the dough onto a lightly floured work surface and knead for about three minutes, or until it becomes smooth. Divide the dough into three equal pieces and form a log measuring approximately twelve inches by 1.5 inches. Transfer the logs to the baking sheet. Brush the top of the logs with the egg white and sprinkle lightly with sugar. Bake the logs in the center of the oven for twenty-five minutes, or until they are lightly browned and slightly firm. Let the logs cool for thirty minutes on the baking sheet. Transfer to cutting board.

Change out the parchment paper with fresh paper. Cut the logs into 1/3-inch slices with a knife. Arrange the biscotti on the sheets, cut sides down, bake, turning once, until golden brown for about 25 minutes.

Alchermes of Florence

https://en.julskitchen.com/drink/home-made-alchermes

Ingredients:

Cinnamon: gr. 12

Coriander: gr. 10

Cochineal: gr. 7

Mace: gr. 3

Cloves: gr. 2.5

Sweet orange peel: gr. 5

Star anise (flowers): gr. 3

Cardamom: 10 grains

Vanilla. half stick

Pure alcohol at 95°: gr. 600

Sugar: gr. 600

Rose water: gr. 100

Instructions:

Crush in the mortar all the herbs (minus the vanilla that you will cut into small pieces) and put everything in a bottle with alcohol and 300 gr. of pure water. Cap the container and leave to infuse for a few weeks, remembering to shake it at least once a day. After this time, cold melt the sugar in half a liter of pure water and add it to the infusion, shake well and leave to rest for another day. Finally, filter the liqueur (with a filter paper cone) and flavor it with rose water.

Alchermes is a Florentine liqueur of very ancient origin. It seems, in fact, that this rosolio was a creation of the Medici family who jealously guarded the recipe. Leo X and Clement VII, both Medici, were fond of it and called it "long life elixir", while in France, where it seems it was brought by Maria de 'Medici and his alchemist Ruggieri, he was known as "Liquore de 'Medici".

Other typical Florence liqueurs are: "L'Acqua di Firenze", based on lemon zest, cloves, cinnamon and nutmeg; the "Fioretto di Firenze" made from Ireos, cinnamon and orange blossom, the "Gemma d'Abeto" from the friars of Monte Senario and the "Certosino" (or Val d'Ema liqueur) from the Certosa di Galluzzo.

Gnudi

Ingredients:

350g firm ricotta

300g cooked, drained and chopped spinach (about 1kg fresh)

2 eggs, beaten

pinch of ground nutmeg

50g plain flour

50g unsalted butter

20 sage leaves

40g grated Parmesan, to serve

Instructions:

Make the gnudi by mixing the ricotta, cooked spinach, and eggs until well combined. Add a pinch of salt and the nutmeg. You should have a thick, compact mixture.

Place the flour in a bowl. With floured hands, roll walnut-sized spoonful of mixture into the flour to coat and then place on a lightly floured plate or board until they are all ready.

Prepare a large pot of simmering, salted water and set over a low heat. Carefully drop the gnudi one by one into the water and cook for 4-5 minutes or until they begin to float.

In the meantime, prepare the sauce by melting the butter in a frying pan. Add the sage leaves and two to three spoonful of the cooking water and swirl the pan to create a thick sauce. Season with salt and pepper.

When the gnudi are ready, remove them from the water with a slotted spoon and place them in the sauce.

Turn the heat to low. Swirl the pan gently to coat the gnudi in the sauce for one minute and serve with the Parmesan cheese.

Farro Salad with Courgetti, Tomato and Mozzarella

https://www.withspice.com/blog/farro-salad-with-zucchini-olives-and-roasted-tomatoes/

Ingredients:

200g farro

1 courgetti, cubed

2 tbsp extra-virgin olive oil, plus extra for drizzling

2 medium tomatoes

1 small red onion, thinly sliced

1 tbsp red-wine vinegar, plus extra for drizzling

1 bunch (about 150g) rocket

10-12 basil leaves, torn

100g fresh mozzarelline (small mozzarella balls, such as bocconcini)

Instructions:

Cook the farro in a large saucepan of boiling water – at least 1 litre – with a pinch of salt. Boil until al dente, about 30 minutes.

Check every now and then – depending on the type of farro, it may take a little less time or a little longer.

Drain the farro and rinse in cold water to cool it down. Set aside to drain and cool completely.

Cook the courgette in the olive oil in a frying pan over a medium heat until golden, 5-7 minutes. Season with a pinch of salt and set aside.

Quarter the tomatoes, remove the seeds and chop the flesh. Set aside.

Place the red-onion slices in a small bowl with the red-wine vinegar and top with cold water – leave to soak for about 10 minutes to take away a little of the bite. Drain when needed.

Combine all the ingredients in a salad bowl. Toss to combine well.

Drizzle with olive oil and red-wine vinegar to taste, and season with salt and pepper.

Florentine Fried Chicken

https://www.academiabarilla.it/en/ricetta/florentine-fried-chicken/

Ingredients:

1kg whole chicken, skin removed

1 rosemary sprig, coarsely chopped

1 bay leaf

1 garlic clove, sliced

juice of 1 lemon

1 liter olive oil, plus extra for coating

125g plain flour for dusting

2 eggs, beaten

Instructions:

Chop the chicken into 18 pieces – four from the leg/thigh, two from the wings, and three from each breast.

Place in a bowl with the rosemary, bay leaf, garlic, lemon juice and enough olive oil to coat the chicken – about 90ml. Marinate for at least one hour.

Remove the chicken from the marinade. Dust the chicken pieces with flour.

Shake off the excess, then dip into the egg and place on a plate ready for deep-frying.

Preheat the oven to 140C/gas mark 1.

Heat the olive oil in a saucepan to 160C. If you don't have a sugar thermometer, test the temperature by throwing in a little cube of bread. It should turn golden in about 20 seconds. Fry in two batches.

After five minutes, turn the heat down to 140C and cook for 10 minutes, turning up the heat again for the last minute for a deep-brown color.

Drain the chicken on paper towel, place in a baking dish and keep warm in the oven, covered in foil, while you're frying the rest.

Season the fried chicken with salt just before serving.

Italian Apple Cake

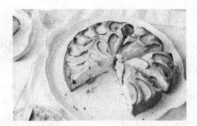

https://www.prouditaliancook.com/2018/10/tuscan-apple-cake.html

Ingredients:

2 large Golden Delicious apples (or other good cooking apple), peeled, cored, and sliced 1cm thick

juice and zest of 1 lemon

180g sugar

125g unsalted butter, softened

3 eggs

150ml milk

300g plain flour

1 tsp baking powder

Instructions:

Preheat the oven to 180C/160C fan/Gas 4. Grease and line a 23cm cake tin.

Place the apple in a bowl with the lemon juice and two tablespoons of the sugar.

Beat the remaining sugar with the butter until pale and creamy, add the eggs and beat very well until you have a thick, pale mixture.

Add the milk and the zest, then fold in the flour, baking powder, a pinch of salt and half the apple slices, along with the lemon juice to combine.

Pour into the cake tin and place the remaining apple slices all over the surface.

Bake in the oven for one hour, or until the top is golden brown and springy to the touch.

Tuscan Style Roasted Leg of Lamb

https://leitesculinaria.com/244823/recipes-tuscan-style-roasted-leg-lamb.html

Ingredients:

5 cloves garlic, crushed

2 tsp sea salt

¼ cup coarsely chopped fresh rosemary

Finely grated zest of one lemon

3 TBSP extra virgin olive oil

3 TBSP fresh lemon juice

1.5 tsp freshly ground black pepper

1 semi-boneless Leg of Lamb (about 7 pounds), with leg bone

1 lemon, cut into thin round slices

Fresh rosemary to garnish

Instructions:

For the marinade

On a cutting board, coarsely chop the crushed garlic. Sprinkle with the salt and then finely chop and, using the flat side of the knife, smear the garlic into a coarse paste.

Add the rosemary and lemon zest and continue chopping and scraping until well combined. Transfer to a small bowl and stir in the oil, lemon juice, and pepper to make a thin paste. (Alternatively, you can purée all of the ingredients in a mini food processor.)

Place the lamb on a large, rimmed baking sheet. Using the tip of a small sharp knife, pierce the lamb about 15 times, making slits about 1 inch (25 mm) wide and deep all over the lamb.

Using a small spoon and your fingertips, fill each slit with some of the rosemary paste. Slather the remaining rosemary paste all over the lamb. Cover with plastic wrap and refrigerate for at least 4 hours or overnight. Remove from the refrigerator and let stand at room temperature for 1 hour to remove its chill before cooking.

For the lamb

Position a rack in the bottom third of the oven and preheat the oven to 400°F (200°C).

Place the lamb in a large roasting pan and roast for 15 minutes.

Reduce the oven temperature to 350°F (177°C). Continue roasting until an instant-read thermometer inserted in the thickest part of the lamb (not touching a bone) reads 130°F (55°C) for medium rare, about 1 1/4 hours. During the last 20 minutes of roasting, arrange the lemon slices on top of the lamb.

Transfer the lamb to a carving board and let rest for 10 to 15 minutes. Set the lemon slices aside.

Using the leg bone as a handle, carve the lamb by slicing vertically along the roast in the boneless area, then parallel to the bone in the shank section.

Transfer the slices to a platter and pour the carving juices on top. Garnish with the rosemary sprigs and lemon slices and serve.

Tuscan Style Roasted Potatoes

https://www.afamilyfeast.com/tuscan-roasted-potatoes

Ingredients:

2 pounds new red potatoes, unpeeled and cut into 1- to-2-inch pieces

¼ cup extra virgin olive oil plus 2 tablespoons to brush the pan

1/3 cup white wine

2 tablespoons garlic, minced

1 teaspoon salt

¼ teaspoon freshly ground black pepper

1 tablespoon chopped fresh sage

1 tablespoon chopped fresh rosemary

Salt to taste

Instructions:

Preheat oven to 425 degrees.

Cut potatoes and put into a large enough bowl to mix. Add oil, wine, garlic, salt, pepper, sage and rosemary. Toss all ingredients to coat potatoes.

Pour onto a sheet pan and place in oven. Potatoes should be close but not touching to get proper browning. a typical 9 X 12 sheet pan is perfect.

Roast for 25 minutes and remove from oven. Using a spatula, turn potatoes and return to oven.

Cook for an additional 20-25 minutes or until potatoes are crispy. Cooking time will vary depending on accuracy of oven and size of potatoes. For our photo, we cut them on the larger size, and it took an additional 15 minutes to get the right degree of browning. The trick is to get the potato tender before the liquid evaporates and then brown until done without burning the herbs. The final 10-15 minutes are crucial to the perfect potato.

Remove from oven and adjust seasoning by adding more salt if needed and serve.

Tuscan Sausage Pasta

https://www.saltandlavender.com/tuscan-sausage-pasta

Ingredients:

8 ounces uncooked pasta (I used fettuccine)

10.6 ounces Italian sausages crumbled

3 cloves garlic minced

1/2 cup chicken broth or dry white wine

1/2 teaspoon Dijon mustard

1 teaspoon flour

1 teaspoon lemon juice

1/4 cup sun-dried tomatoes

1 cup heavy/whipping cream

1.5 cups baby spinach (loosely packed)

Small handful fresh basil chopped finely

Salt & pepper to taste

Freshly grated parmesan cheese to taste

Instructions:

Boil a salted pot of water and cook pasta al dente according to package directions.

Take the sausages out of their casings and crumble the meat into a skillet. Sauté over medium-high heat for 5 minutes, stirring occasionally, until it's nicely browned on the outside.

Remove the sausage from the pan and set aside. If there's a lot of fat, discard most of it.

Add the garlic, chicken broth, Dijon mustard, flour, and lemon juice to the pan. Stir until well combined (be sure to scrape up any brown bits from the bottom of the pan) and let it bubble for a minute or two.

Add the sun-dried tomatoes and cream to the pan. Let it cook for 2-3 minutes.

Add the sausage back into the pan. Cook for another few minutes until the sauce has thickened up a bit.

Stir in the basil and spinach. Let it cook for a minute or so until it wilts. Give the sauce a taste and season with extra salt & pepper if needed.

Drain the pasta and toss it with the sauce. Serve immediately with some freshly grated parmesan if desired.